FORGOTTEN QUEEN

VASILISA DRAKE

CONTENTS

To anyone who has hurt someone they love.

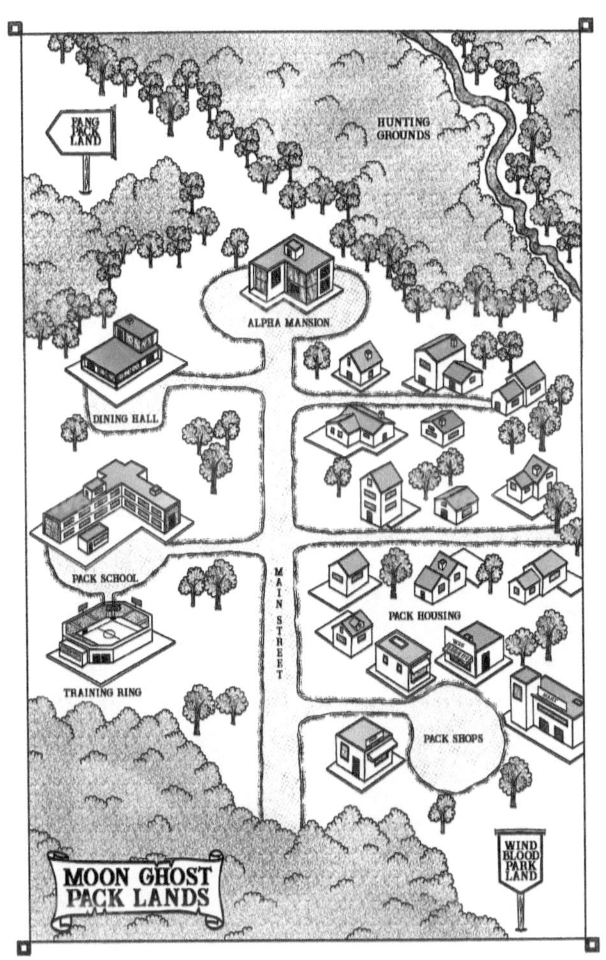

FANG PACK LAND
HUNTING GROUNDS
ALPHA MANSION
DINING HALL
PACK SCHOOL
TRAINING RING
MAIN STREET
PACK HOUSING
PACK SHOPS
WIND BLOOD PARK LAND
MOON GHOST PACK LANDS

CHAPTER I

I STUMBLED OUT OF the portal and onto the ground.

More accurately, I dropped out of the portal twenty feet above the ground and crashed onto the forest floor.

Ow.

My head spun as it tried to catch up to my sudden journey. The ringing in my ears drowned out everything for a long moment. *Inhale, exhale.* Deep breaths as I adjusted. The experience was utterly disorienting.

I flipped over in time to catch the fading yellow sparks as the portal disappeared.

My hands sank into a layer of snow on the ground as I forced myself up to take in my surroundings. The icy sensation slammed into my core. I still wore my cloak, which provided some protection from the winter chill, but not much. Of course, when you get used to being surrounded by a moat of lava, your tolerance for the cold gets diminished.

I'd died—been murdered—and gone to the afterlife. In my time in Hell, I'd faced demons, trained with a witch, and been turned to stone. I had no idea how long I'd been there. Time had lost meaning. And now... I was *back*.

Part of me was convinced I was still in Hell, that the Libra demon hadn't actually held up his end of the deal—that I had no plans of fulfilling my part of—but a glance up at the sky confirmed it was the navy of night, not the crimson of Hell. The air itself tasted different. Familiar, like a distant memory of home.

I pinched myself to be sure. The icy pinch didn't change the sight in front of me.

Snow on the ground. Trees. A waxing crescent moon above.

I was here.

Of course, the question was—where *was* here?

I'd given Phaidros, the demon who opened the portal, instructions to drop me off on Moon-Ghost pack lands, but he hadn't exactly used a GPS.

Ugh. I had to hope I was somewhere nearby, but I didn't recognize my surroundings as pack lands. And I'd never been allowed off of them, never seen the bordering territories.

I bit down a growl of frustration. *Think, Avery, think.* Every moment spent wasted was a moment my best friend suffered. I *had* to get to Daphne.

I looked up at the sky. The night was clear, not a single cloud marring the stars decorating the sky. I'd spent a lot of nights hiding on rooftops from the Alpha Clique, watching the stars. Daphne had spent many of those nights with me.

The memories were a spiked pang in my chest, squeezing at the wound of loneliness.

I knew the sky in Moon-Ghost territory. It was similar, but not quite a match for what was above me. I was a bit too far south. At least, I was mostly sure about that.

Before I'd died, I'd have said a prayer to the Moon Goddess that I was correct, beseeched her to guide my steps.

But I couldn't force myself to believe in her tonight. Not after who she'd given me for a fated mate.

So, now, I had to trust *myself*. I picked a direction and set off.

I hadn't walked for ten minutes before a growl cut through the night.

Shifter.

The scent of a wolf—no, wolves—arrived on the air a short moment later, serving as confirmation.

Shit. In a split second, I considered and dismissed the possibility of running. They knew where I was, and they were willing to chase me.

Three massive wolves emerged from the shadows, spreading around me. Not a sneak attack, but a direct confrontation. A patrol.

I didn't recognize the three ash-furred wolves, which meant they didn't recognize me, hopefully. Strangers might be dangerous, but it was my own pack that had killed me. It was around them I'd need to be most careful.

If I made it that far.

The wolf in the center growled again.

It wasn't possible to speak as a wolf, but the demand in his voice was a clear threat. I was an intruder on their territory. *Not that I'd be welcomed on what had been my own.*

I couldn't afford the delay.

"I'm just passing through. I'll be gone by morning," I said, hoping to placate them. The growling didn't stop. Worse, the other two joined in. "What do you want from me?" I snapped. It's not like I could make my own portal, dammit.

But my answer didn't please the patrol. The largest wolf in the center snarled.

And then he launched himself at me.

I shifted on sheer instinct, shedding my human skin as easily as I did the cloak I'd worn. I darted aside in the nick of time.

Guess I didn't lose all the strength I gained in Hell. It had been a gamble whether returning to Earth would condemn me back to my weak body. But I was strong. Steady. In tune with my wolf.

I didn't have time to be glad for my luck though, because even if I was now as strong as a normal shifter, I was outnumbered and surrounded. A second wolf slammed into my right flank, trying to bring me down with brute force. I twisted, clawing his muzzle.

The scent of blood coated the air. The first drops had

spilled. And they only seemed to whet the patrol's appetite.

Shit.

And worse than anything, I didn't want to kill them. They were just wolves doing their duty to protect their pack. A bit aggressive, but I was an unknown intruder. They had packmates, families to protect.

It was that thought that had me trying to dodge rather than strike back.

But my opponents didn't seem to have any such hesitation. They were relentless.

Claws and teeth. Blood and fur. Our snarls stopped only long enough to wrap our jaws around each other.

But it was over when one landed a massive swipe on my side while I had one of the other's leg in my mouth and tried to claw the third.

I gave as good as I got for every hit, but the three closed in around me. No chance to escape. I was cornered.

The largest gray wolf charged, pinning me, slamming me into a tree. The large gash I'd taken at my side, so reminiscent of the one I'd been dealt at the end of my life, drained the last of my strength.

The once pure white snow was painted red with my blood.

And then darkness claimed me.

CHAPTER II

I CAME TO SLOWLY, pain ricocheting through every inch of my body.

I forced my eyelids open, trying to take in my surroundings as quickly as I could despite every protest my body emitted.

My body was covered with animal pelts, the furs a warm barrier against the winter chill. I must've been in a cabin. The walls were simple wooden logs. Somewhere behind me, a fire crackled, warming the air around me.

But any further surveillance of my surroundings was cut short as I met the gaze of two peridot eyes.

"You're finally awake."

He was a tall male, around my age, if a few years older. I inhaled his scent, matching it to memory immediately.

I still had the taste of his blood on my teeth. He'd been the largest wolf, the one who led the confrontation.

"You knocked me out," I accused. It was hardly fair to hold that against me since he was the cause of my blood loss.

How much time have I lost?

"By right, I could have killed you," the male snapped back.

He wasn't wrong, so I said nothing to that. "And if I deem you a threat to my pack, as the Alpha Heir, I'll do just that."

Another day, another death threat. That wasn't even worth noticing. Aside from Jett, I knew little of the other Alpha Heirs. I'd assumed any alive weren't of age. "I didn't see you at the Choosing," I said, continuing my thoughts aloud.

"Six months ago, I was otherwise occupied."

I had to fight a gasp, if only because the start of the inhale sent a new wave of pain firing through my chest. *Six months had gone by?* I knew time had passed; the snow attested to that, but I'd hoped for the beginning of winter, not the end.

The male—the Alpha Heir—read something in my expression, but there was no way he could guess the truth. He frowned, the corners of his mouth turning sour.

"What were you doing trespassing on our land?" he demanded.

Well, gee, I stumbled through a portal and the demon didn't exactly pick the right spot to dump me.

"I got lost," I settled on. I didn't have a better excuse.

This had to be Wind-Blood pack land, at least based on my surroundings. They were more developed than Moon-Ghost gossip led us to believe—I supposed the shirtless, oiled prancing was just for show at the ceremony. The Fangs were distinct for their biker club home base. The black leather and roar of motorcycles didn't mesh with the minimalistic cabin.

The heir was clearly dissipated by my explanation. He narrowed his eyes at me, like that would coax more answers. "Spy?"

"Ah, yes, you caught me. Rule one of being a spy: admit it when questioned," I said, unable to help the sarcasm that infected my voice.

Okay, maybe mouthing off to my captor wasn't a good idea, but hopefully, he didn't really want to kill me since he'd brought me back to his camp rather than leaving me to bleed out in the snow after maiming me. And truly, I'd had enough cowering for a lifetime—literally.

He was at least reasonable enough to recognize it as a dumb question. "Fine. Who's your pack?"

I could lie and say Fangs or admit to having been part of Moon-Ghost. Both carried risks.

"Why?" I asked, fishing for more context of how he felt.

His glare offered no answers.

If he was looking to figure out my pack to return me to them and I said the Fangs, they'd know I lied and might rip me apart on principle.

Honestly, I was never built for subterfuge. "I was part of Moon-Ghost."

"Was?"

"I was cast out." No grief accompanied my words. The wound had healed. I never would find companionship there. But anger, oh yes, that coated my words.

Questions creased his brow, but they were cut off as someone else entered the room. I still couldn't sit up to see, only twist my head toward the faint sound of footsteps on the dirt floor, but whoever they belonged to was just out of my view.

"You're upsetting my patient." The new voice was strong, authoritative.

"She could be a Moon-Ghost spy," the heir protested.

The other shifter came into view. Her hair was braided silver, stray wisps framing her face. Her skin was parchment-thin, yet she looked anything but frail. There was muscle to her, at least from what I could see of her bare arms. For a shifter to show their age like that, she had to be a pack elder.

She cast a scathing look towards the heir. It almost reminded me of Hecate, though the two women didn't resemble each other in the slightest.

Of course, the thought of Hecate threatened to release an onslaught of others. Thoughts of him. So many secrets I needed to unravel. But all that came second to rescuing Daphne.

"Yes, I can see she's about to leap off the table and uncover our secrets, Xander." The sarcasm dripped off her tongue as she chastised the heir—Xander. "She's hardly in any shape to do any spying. You three nearly tore her whole flank apart."

I grimaced at her description of my condition. It took all of my strength to raise my arm enough to get a glance under the blanket while she shooed the Alpha Heir away. She overruled his protests with the ease of someone who had known the male since he was a pup.

I winced when I saw what lay beneath. It was brutal. I looked more like a mauled animal, barely held together by a thread, than a whole person. Wounds taken in shifter form translated to the human shape. I knew that. But of course, having never spent much time in my wolf form, I'd never realized the brutality that would translate to.

My hand was suddenly swatted, my arm crashing down as that little bit of strength was depleted.

The elder turned her flinty eyes on me. "Don't undo all my hard work by ripping your stitches. The poultice can only do so much if you agitate it."

It seemed silly, but it wasn't until then I realized my right side was entirely numb. No doubt the work of whatever she'd treated me with.

"Why are you helping me?" I asked.

The flint in her eyes softened. "It's not my nature to let wolves die needlessly."

"But it was your pack who attacked me."

She waved a dismissive hand. "The young ones are on edge." I supposed even though he was a full-fledged adult, the heir was little more than a pup in her eyes. "They're overzealous in their attempts to protect the pack. Bear no grudge against them."

Bear no grudge after they ripped out my side? Yet, truly, I didn't, and they'd brought me back to be healed after all.

"Why are they on edge?" I probed.

The elder moved along my body, poking and prodding as she assessed what was presumably her own handiwork. "This world is out of balance. It began ages ago, a slight tilt that began to push us toward our demise. Then, something changed. A twist in destiny. I sense it, as do the other elders of Wind-Blood. It gets under your fur, distorts sensations until you're teetering on the edge."

I was torn between the urge to dismiss her ramblings as nonsense or take them seriously. I'd learned the afterlife was real—and not just the "cast among the stars" vagueness we learned as part of shifter lore. Magic, murderous mermaids, creatures that turned you to stone with a glance. So it wasn't out of the realm of possibility that there was some truth to what the elder said.

Of course, if it was true, that meant more trouble was brewing.

Still, I couldn't let that concern me. What I needed was to get out of this cabin, out of Wind-Blood lands, and break Daphne out of the Moon-Ghost cells. I wasn't sure if they'd help me—or rather, if they'd try to keep me here. But I needed to go as soon as my body could carry me.

If the gentle clicking of her tongue was any indication, I was in bad shape.

And the elder was thorough. She worked her way up my body, going so far as to press her fingers through my hair to check my scalp. The red strands of my hair fell forward as she examined me.

Her fingers twisted through, and she bent low, her head inches above my forehead as she looked.

"Um, everything okay?" I asked, slightly edging farther down on the table. "Ouch!"

The exclamation came as she yanked on my hair, plucking a strand out.

She walked past me and held the strand up to the fading light of a window across the room, then spun back to face me.

"You've returned."

CHAPTER III

I FROWNED. *DID SHE know I'd come back from Hell?*

"It's been many years since the red wolf walked... many of the others have forgotten." She seemed to be talking to herself more than me, her eyes taking on a distant look, but the words just confused me more. "The pups didn't recognize the significance when they dragged you to my table."

For the elder to appear as she did, she had to be old. I guessed easily over a hundred, though it was hard to say with any more precision because Moon-Ghost didn't really *have* elders.

"What are you talking about?" I asked.

She returned my frown, her brows creased as she read my face. "There is an old tale, one whispered in shadows on moonless nights. Of a red wolf and a black wolf." She gestured to my hair.

What was she talking about? My red fur was unusual—there were no other shifters with it that I'd ever met, but Moon-Ghost didn't comprise every single wolf ever. It had been a source of torment, a mark that I was different.

But red and black... I cast my mind back, remembering a mural I'd seen in the dim light of the castle dungeon. Two wolves had been there too. I hadn't had time to think about it—being petrified immediately after would do that—but in the back of my mind, I'd wondered.

"One ruled over life, the other death," she continued. "And together, they ruled all of us."

A black wolf... *Cole.*

Cole, who I'd left behind in Hell, who had a barrage of secrets he'd been keeping. Who I'd kissed. Who I'd poisoned. Who infected my dreams and had watched me for years. I hadn't seen him when I was asleep, but maybe that was simply because I hadn't been asleep so much as passed out from blood loss.

Once again, I was left with more questions, but I had to focus on one thing at a time. If she believed I was related to whatever red wolf she spoke about so reverently, maybe she'd help me.

"Look, my friend is trapped in a Moon-Ghost cell," I said urgently. "I need to get to her."

The reverence disappeared, and the appraising eyes of the healer returned. "You won't be going anywhere soon. You'll require at least a week to recover. If you'd been human, you'd be dead."

If that was my yardstick, then it was a miracle I was as good as I was since I'd barely been a half-step above human when

I'd last walked on the Earth. Somehow, dying had righted something inside me.

"Is there anything you can do?" I pleaded.

The woman shook her head, and any further conversation was cut off as the door swung open.

"The Alpha wishes to see you," Xander announced. "I'll stay with the she-wolf." I guessed my reprieve was done.

"Then I'll attend to my son," the healer said in parting. My eyes went wide. She wasn't just a pack elder, but the former Alpha female and grandmother to Xander, who now stood over me, his arms crossed in an imposing manner that I struggled to take seriously.

"Can I help you?" I said testily. He was just *looking* at me.

"Not sure I trust you to be left alone, no matter what she says."

I don't trust anyone. I bit down on the words. I wanted to confide in someone, but I'd have to be delusional to do so with the Wind-Blood Heir.

Instead, I turned my gaze to the rest of the room, casting about for a conversation topic. "It's not what I expected."

It was more rustic than what we had in the Moon-Ghost village, but all I knew about the Wind-Bloods came from idle pack gossip and seeing them the one time at the full moon, gleaming in oil and bathing in moonlight.

He arched a brow at me. "Did you expect dirt floors and little huts?"

"Kinda," I admitted, embarrassed. Wind-Bloods were fast, strong wolves, but primitive, according to Moon-Ghost sources. In contrast, the Fangs lived almost fully in human society, nearly suffocating their wolf sides. Only the Moon-Ghosts had achieved a proper balance.

By isolating ourselves and refusing to socialize with the other packs outside of the moon-matching ceremony.

In hindsight, that view was probably more than a *little* biased.

As if reading my thoughts, Xander rolled his eyes. "Just because we honor the old traditions doesn't mean we're savages."

Maddox, the Moon-Ghost Alpha, had always derided them as bloodthirsty fanatics specifically. Yet, I knew with full confidence if Moon-Ghost had found a stray wolf on their lands, that wolf wouldn't have survived the confrontation, let alone be brought back to get patched up.

I pressed a hand to my side, exploring the sensation. It went two ways: numb when I didn't touch it and blistering, blindingly painful when I did. The movement caused the fur blanket on me to fall off my shoulder, catching Xander's eyes.

Acutely aware of my nudity, I flushed. Shifters should be comfortable naked since the shift itself tended to destroy any clothing, but I'd missed that part of socialization growing up and was self-conscious. Xander's gaze was proper shifter, not lingering, utterly unaffected by my exposed body. It was only a mild comfort.

"Could I possibly get some clothes?" I asked him.

"And ruin the view?" The taunt was empty of any sexual innuendo; his attention focused on my eyes. "Besides, you'd ruin my grandmother's hard work by tearing your stitches if you tried to put anything on."

I didn't have the energy to mount an argument.

Xander moved across the room, dragging a chair from somewhere out of view towards me. He picked up a book and started to read, though I couldn't look down to see just what he was looking at.

"Has it really been six months?" I asked after a few moments of silence, still trying to process.

"Since what?"

"The Choosing." The night that had changed everything.

"Did you not have a calendar? Even us backwater Wind-Bloods have those," he teased.

Though he clearly didn't trust me—which was fair, since I was technically an intruder, even if it was unintentional—he wasn't so bad. Maybe there was truth to what the pack elder had said about the wolves being on edge because I couldn't reconcile his ruthless attack with his easy teasing and reading while he "guarded" his prisoner.

"No," I answered. "Not where I was."

He took that as an opportunity for an interrogation, but I had no answers to give him. I couldn't tell him I was in Hell.

When that was a dead end, he shifted gears, asking me about Moon-Ghost. I gave some general information—I didn't feel an overabundance of loyalty to my old pack, but I didn't feel compelled to help Xander either. He tried to grill me for what I knew about Wind-Blood or even the Fangs, but it was clear he knew more than I did. Moon-Ghost had been more isolationist than I'd realized.

Xander wasn't bad company, but what I needed was time to figure out how to get to Daphne.

When everyone fell asleep, I'd hoped to sneak out, but I had no way to do that with my side being the way it was.

And if I didn't manage that, I would have to sleep as well.

I dreaded what—or who—I'd find there.

CHAPTER IV

I DREADED FALLING ASLEEP that night.

For years, my dreams had been my only true respite from the unending bullying I faced in the pack. There was a voice, a male one I'd dismissed as my subconsciousness's cure to my crippling loneliness.

All too late, I'd realized the voice belonged to Cole.

I'd seen the face of the voice once as a pup, but somehow he'd hidden himself since. Of course, I'd assumed it was my imagination, a fictitious friend and my only companion besides Daphne.

Yet, when I'd died and wound up in Hell, I hadn't connected the impossible fact. It had been more than a decade since the glimpse of his face I'd long since dismissed as a dream. How was I to know the arrogant, demanding Alpha was the same soothing voice that had comforted me through broken bones and other humiliations?

But he was more than a simple voice, much more. Our connection made no sense.

He'd told me I was once his queen.

And right now, he was furious with me for escaping.

I mean, it didn't help I'd kissed him, dosing him with poison and knocking him out. It had been the hottest kiss of my life (or undeath) until he'd slumped in my arms.

He said there'd be consequences. No doubt he would make me pay for the betrayal.

I dreaded finding him in my dreams, but my body could no longer stand to stay awake. My body might be numb to pain, but I was beyond exhausted from the blood loss. Though I hadn't tracked the hours, I'd had precious little rest since escaping his castle in Hell.

Sleep was inevitable, no matter how I fought it. So I let myself give in.

But my dreams were silent.

When I woke, I was almost disappointed. I might not be able to trust Cole, but my wolf had found a companion in him.

The darkness outside the window told me I'd woken up far sooner than I'd planned. Likely, I'd only dozed for a few hours. I twisted my head as far as I could, not seeing any other shapes in the darkness. Xander must've figured I wasn't going anywhere overnight.

A week, the healer had told me.

The image of Daphne rose from my memory unbidden, bile in my throat following it. My best friend crouched in a filthy cell with a threadbare blanket barely covering her as she shivered. What crime could she have possibly committed to warrant such treatment? Her father was the pack Beta, so if his daughter was treated like that despite his influence, there was no telling how much worse it might get. My chest tightened.

I didn't have a week.

The sleep had restored enough of my mental faculties to plan at least. In life, I'd been a scrawny, below-average wolf. The pack Omega who couldn't shift right.

Yet, since returning from Hell, something in me was fixed. I could shift as well as, if not better than, the average wolf. My training had stayed with me.

But it wasn't only shifter training I'd done in the underworld.

No, there was also witchcraft.

I hadn't been exactly gifted despite what Hecate claimed, and I'd never tried anything like this.

But it *had* to work. I refused to even contemplate failure.

I shut my eyes and focused. I needed my body to fix itself. I needed that with a desperation I'd never felt before. Because it wasn't my life on the line, it was Daphne's.

I focused my thoughts on memories of my best friend. Us sitting on rooftops gazing up at stars. Running from the Alpha Clique. Trying on clothes, laughing at whatever pack gossip was particularly entertaining that day.

Friendship was a powerful force. I willed my magic to

channel that force and mend itself.

Sweat trickled down the side of my forehead as I scrunched my face in focus.

The numbness was the first to go. I bit my tongue so hard I tasted blood in my effort to stop crying out. I'd thought merely tapping my side before was painful? This was an ocean of agony. It pulsed like a living, vicious thing, rounding through me in waves.

I wanted to give in. To stop trying.

But that wasn't an option.

Daphne. I focused on the memories of my friend.

And then... the blistering pain eased.

Not a lot. A fraction of relief that barely made a dent, but it was enough to bolster my efforts.

Heal, damn it!

It wasn't instantaneous. The process was an eternity.

But eventually, the pain faded. I rubbed my sides, the movement no longer painful, marveling at the unblemished skin my fingers met under the fur blanket.

For the first time all day, I had enough strength to sit up. The movement was nearly effortless compared to before. I examined my body with my own eyes. The stitches had disappeared like magic, which was good because I didn't relish the thought of pulling them out of my newly healed skin.

It wasn't perfect. The skin was healed, but underneath was tender, like a brutal bruise lay hidden.

But I could move.

I could escape.

I glanced around, better able to appreciate my surroundings. The barest moonlight lit the room from one faraway window, but it was enough for my honed senses to make out the contents of the room. No one was here. I stepped off the sick bed as quietly as if I was sneaking past the Alpha Clique in the hallways as a youth. It was a good thing I'd been used to avoiding detection.

My attention caught on a bundle of clothes in the chair next to me, the one Xander had dragged across the dirt floor to read in. Clothes. He'd brought them despite his initial refusal. No doubt he hadn't planned on me escaping in them, but with the winter chill, I was grateful.

I dressed and slowly opened the cabin door, grateful for the well-oiled hinges. I opened it the barest fraction to strain my hearing to listen outside, but all signs showed the Wind-Blood camp was silent.

I eased my body outside and read the sky. I had a better sense of where I was now. My travels to Moon-Ghost would be much easier once I crossed into the territory, which was to the northwest of Wind-Blood territory.

I had no desire to linger and get caught again. This time, I'd be more careful, sticking to trees if I needed to. Still, curiosity gnawed at me. This would likely be my only opportunity to ever see the Wind-Blood camp. Much of it matched the cabin I'd been in, simple wood lodges lining the camp, which was sheltered by a nearby mountain. Rather than wandering through the seemingly empty camp, I scaled the side of the one I'd been in so I could cross the rooftops.

From my vantage there, the path was clearer. I just needed to get to the tree line.

I padded as quietly as I could across the roof before jumping to the next, landing easily on the pads of my feet. One by one, I crossed, refusing to sacrifice my silent travels for speed. I may have healed myself, but I wasn't going to count on being able to do so again.

There. The tree line was thirty feet away.

Twenty.

Ten.

I lowered myself from the roof of the cabin on the edge, avoiding any windows as I landed on the snow.

Five more feet and I could get into the forest and continue my journey.

"Going somewhere?"

CHAPTER V

*C*AUGHT.

Xander leaned against the cabin I'd just jumped down from, having hidden himself around the corner of it. His hands were folded over his chest, eyes unreadable.

"I have to get to my friend." My words were soft, not wanting to rouse any half-asleep shifters, but strong.

"You must be pretty determined if you're able to even move after the wounds you had."

I shrugged, edging back slightly, away from the camp. I didn't need our voices carrying. "Guess I heal fast."

His eyes narrowed, but he didn't call me on it.

Instead, he stepped forward. I refused to yield, even to the Wind-Blood Alpha Heir, by stepping back again.

"You must really care for this friend," he said.

"She's all I have." My voice cracked, but I held his gaze.

He glanced away, his posture softening.

"You kept asking about the Choosing," he said, changing to a subject that made the hair on the back of my neck stand on end. "You know I wasn't there, but it caused quite a stir.

Your pack Alpha's brat son found his fated mate. He forsook her."

I kept silent, not liking where he was going with this.

"He rejected his fated mate," he repeated when I didn't say anything. "And then, in a sin beyond any other, he killed her."

Still, I didn't speak.

"Her body wasn't found, of course, but Moon-Ghost declared her dead. It caused quite a stir, shedding blood on one of our holiest nights. The other Alphas were furious. It was a violation of everything the ceremony stands for."

He leaned forward as if seeing me properly for the first time.

"But if that wolf didn't die... if that wolf escaped..." His voice was almost gentle. "Well, let's say that wolf could find allies in the Wind-Bloods, should she ever need them."

Gratitude flooded through me.

"If I ever see that wolf, I'll be sure to let her know," I whispered.

Xander nodded once. Then turned his back on me, heading back to the center of camp, where chimney smoke warmed the air.

A cold wind cut through the forest. I knew Moon-Ghost lay to the northwest, though it would be a long journey from the heart of Wind-Blood territory.

I didn't have time to waste.

I had to move quickly, which, despite my miraculous healing, hurt. My entire side was one big bruise brewing, but it was leagues better than my organs being one thin strand of string from spilling out.

I wanted to get away from the Wind-Blood turf fast. Even if Xander was letting me go with this blessing, I didn't need another "communication issue" ruining my exit. I booked it. Not quite a sprint, but I set off in a fast-paced jog, desperate to reach my best friend. The miles burned under my feet as hours passed. At another time, I might've enjoyed the freedom that came from running through the forest.

Now, I was on a mission.

I reached the river that served as the boundary between Moon-Ghost and Wind-Blood territory. It wasn't huge, maybe twelve feet across with some stones dotting the water that would make passage possible.

I wanted to continue, but that wouldn't be wise.

There was no way I could sneak into the center of Moon-Ghost territory in broad daylight.

The decision not to cross yet was logical, but it didn't come easily.

Here, downwind of Moon-Ghost with the river scent to mask me, I was still hidden even if a patrol came nearby. Not that it was likely anyone was looking for me. After all, Xander had told me I—or rather, Jett's mate—had been declared dead. Ideally, I'd have wanted to wait right outside the town until it was time to act, but that was too dangerous.

I'd need to wait until the early hours of the evening to finish my journey and sneak in under the cover of darkness. At the pace I'd been going, the town should be just about two hours away. Maybe a little longer since I'd need to go slowly, hiding from any other patrols.

I'd learned my lesson with the Wind-Bloods after all. They'd caught me off guard, still half-dazed from my time in Hell, but I'd been lucky.

I didn't count on that luck holding.

I climbed a nearby tree with thick branches. There was no way I could risk sleeping on the forest floor. The inherent risk of the tree was that I would move and fall in my sleep, but it was the lesser of two evils, so that's what I picked.

I rested my eyes before sleeping, putting together my plan. The Moon-Ghost cells, I'd recognized, even though I'd never been in them myself. The Alpha, Maddox King, kept them under his house. Actually, I think the cells predated the house. I'd never heard of them being used. After all, Moon-Ghost didn't hesitate to kill intruders. We'd been taught about the cells in school, and Jett King had bragged about seeing them and how any wolf who tried to harm the pack would rot down there.

The teachers hadn't corrected him.

I'd never heard of anyone invading us, though. I assumed they were just remnants of a different time. The three packs had a somewhat easy truce, each keeping to their own territory.

I'd asked my mother—one of the rare times she'd been home and sober—about them. That had ended her sobriety for the evening, as she'd popped the first of many beers immediately after asking. No pleading would stop her or allow me to recant my question. She told me stories of horrible tortures Maddox would do to those he placed in those cells. She did so in enough excruciating detail I hadn't slept soundly for an entire week.

I rarely thought of my mother. Mainly because I suspected she rarely thought of me. She hadn't even come to the Choosing, which should've been one of her momentous nights as a parent. It was hard to tell if part of why I was targeted was because my mother would rather get plastered than defend her pup or if I was such a failure that I drove her to drink more.

Maybe she was relieved when I'd died. We'd been strangers inhabiting the same house at different hours for years by the time I was twenty. I was a consequence of one of many indiscretions. My father, I was sure, was just as ashamed. Whoever he was, he'd never claimed me.

Enough. Focus on Daphne. I didn't know why Daphne was in the cells, but it didn't matter. What mattered was that I needed to get to her. Unfortunately, the only surefire way I knew would be to go through the King's house.

If this had been a full moon night, it'd be easy. Just wait

until everyone was out of the house on a pack run. Sneaking in while the Kings were sleeping was a hair less dangerous than strolling through in broad daylight.

I wished I had the books from Cole's library. Maybe one of them would hold an answer, offer some plants I could use like I had with Cole. I knew there were plants, but finding them and preparing them just the right way would be impossible without the guidebook.

There was no sense ruminating on it, though. The best thing I could do was get a few hours of rest, allowing my body to heal what the magic hadn't quite managed, and be ready to rescue Daphne.

So I slept.

And this time, I dreamed.

I was on a small island, if it could even be called that. The whole thing was maybe twenty feet in diameter. Water surrounded me on all sides, with no other land as far as the eye could see. The sky burned a brilliant red, revealing the truth of my location.

Being in Hell had made my dreams screwy, but sleeping on Earth was like all those dreams I'd had through adolescence. The scene was familiar. In the past, the settings had varied wildly, but now, I realized all of them were parts of Hell.

"Show yourself," I demanded. Cole must've been around, and I wasn't going to act scared of him.

Even if I might have a very good reason to. A pissed-off Cole was a dangerous thing. And I suspected it was much worse than that.

"I know you're out there, Cole," I said when only silence greeted me. "Face me, dammit!"

"Looking for me, little wolf?"

I spun to face the source of the noise and nearly slammed into Cole. He'd suddenly appeared right behind me. His hands snapped to my wrists, catching me as I stumbled off balance.

I should've shaken off his grip, but for a moment, all I could do was stare. It had been a matter of days, yet it felt like an eternity since I'd seen him.

His hair was a wild mess of dark curls, nearly covering his eyes, though they did nothing to soften the demanding amber glow that held me in place. He wore one of his more favored outfits, a silk dress shirt that was only half-buttoned, revealing the hint of hair on his chest that was eye level for me, the edges of his mysterious tattoo exposed.

I drank the sight in, yet there was something different about him.

Or maybe I'd never properly seen him.

You heard Hecate call me the King. *His parting words from another dream before I entered the capital rang through. There'd been hints, things Hecate let slip, the castle, the dungeon, all of which I'd ignored until it was impossible.*

"Who are you, Cole?" I asked. I meant the question to be a demand, but it came out as barely more than a whisper.

"The better question, little wolf, is who are you?"

"You called me your queen."

"I said you once were," he corrected.

"What does that mean?" My voice came stronger now, but Cole didn't answer. Just stared down at me in that infuriating way that said I'd get no answers. "Tell me, damn you!" I slammed into his chest, the anger of the secrets cascading over me, and though he didn't stumble, he let me. He let me beat at his chest, pounding, demanding. Tears sprang to my eyes, my vision blurring in the dream. "Why do you have to keep so many secrets?"

Only at this did Cole answer. "The secrets are meant to keep you safe."

Safe? What safety had I ever known?

"Trust me, little wolf."

But I no longer trusted anyone.

CHAPTER VI

A NOISE STARTLED ME away from my argument with Cole. I instinctively stilled, drawing as close as I could to the tree while I listened. Footsteps, two sets, across the water. Loud enough to be heard by shifter hearing over the babble of the river. Whoever it was, they weren't trying to be careful, and more importantly, they were in their human form.

I drew in a steadying breath. My face was dry of tears despite what I'd experienced in my dreams. Once again, Cole had left me with more questions than answers, but I had no doubt I'd be seeing him again.

"Stop being such a little bitch and quit worrying," a female voice ordered.

Sabine.

My body shook instinctively as her shrill tone hit my ears. Sabine had been the worst of my tormentors, part of the Alpha Clique, and she'd been the one to deal the killing blow, tossing me over the cliff under Jett's supervision.

I willed my body to be still and listen.

"I'm not a little bitch," Richard whined, sounding very much like a little girl. So much for the third member of the Alpha Clique. Richard often served as Jett's *de facto* Beta, carrying out his dirty work without question.

Do they know I'm here? Anxiety pulsed through me, the remnant of a decade spent hiding from their sadistic bullying. The brief snippet indicated the contrary, but what were they doing out here?

I must've slept for a while, my weakened body needing any rest it could get. The filtered sun falling through the leaves was a burning orange rather than simple daylight. I needed my two tormentors to leave if I was going to make it to camp.

"You know I'm basically an Alpha, right?" Richard insisted.

"Of course I do." Sabine didn't even bother trying to sound sincere. "You're a big, brawny male, and just what I need."

Big, brawny male was right.

Having them this close, unable to move, was torture. My body wanted to flee; my mind wanted to sink into my memories.

My mind won.

Richard wasn't bright, but he was big and single-minded. Jett and Sabine were the true instigators. Jett liked to know he ruled over someone weak, and Sabine wanted to make sure Jett felt all-powerful. She probably wanted that power to rub off on her.

Richard was a convenient tool, one who'd been given the task of tormenting me. Outside of school, I could usually avoid them. Over the years, I got good at it.

But I hadn't always been so good.

It was hard to believe they held back at all, but as bad as school was, being caught by them outside was worse.

I'd been ten, barely a scrap of a kid. It was a summer day. Not a pleasant one, but one of those festering, humid days where your clothing sticks to your skin and the sun is a torture device. I normally stayed home, but the house was stuffy with the ceiling fans broken once again and my mother nowhere to be seen to fix them.

I'd gone out into the forest, figuring I could find relief in the shade of the forest and the isolation of my thoughts. I didn't have anyone to hang out with—Daphne and I didn't become friends until middle school.

My hearing sucked, which made it easy to sneak up on me, and I was also still a bit naive, unaware of how cruel kids could be. Most adults assumed we'd just eventually figure out the pecking order and everything would be good and well.

"There she is! Grab her," Sabine ordered.

That was the only warning I had before Richard snatched me from where I'd been resting under the shade of a tree.

"What should we do with her?" Richard asked, holding me off the ground with ease. He was just a kid too, but I was scrawny, nothing but skin and bones.

I didn't even try to run. Just shuttered in on myself, pleading with my eyes.

"She's all sweaty and stinks," Sabine said, scrunching her nose and fanning her face.

Jett had met my gaze.

"Take her to the river."

There was a small river that ran through the northeast of pack lands. I couldn't even recall the journey. Some of my memories were like that, blacked-out bits of time, but what came after, I remembered viscerally.

"Since you smell, we should give you a bath," Jett said. "Dunk her."

The order was for Richard. Even at a young age, it was clear Jett would be the next Alpha, and all of our age group obeyed accordingly.

Richard threw me in the water, but if I thought to swim away, it came too late. Richard held my head in a vise while Sabine crouched over me, Jett standing above her, looking down his nose as I was drenched.

"Let me out." It was the first time I'd spoken during the whole interaction. There was a twitch of surprise in Jett's eyes, like he forgot I was capable of speech instead of being a mute prop.

But my plea only delighted Sabine. "Come on, stinky. We're just helping you. You should thank us."

"Yeah, thank us," Jett said.

I kept silent. The water wasn't too deep, but I was barely four feet tall, so I couldn't reach the bottom. Richard's grip kept me above water, but it was extremely painful.

"Dunk her," Jett ordered.

I opened my mouth to protest. A dangerous mistake. Richard obeyed without hesitation, and I got a big mouthful of water. The feeling of choking isn't one you forget. I flailed, desperate. I was nearly convinced I was going to drown there, but they brought me back up.

"Thank us," Jett ordered again.

I sputtered, trying to cough up the water I'd swallowed. The delay in my answer had Richard dunking me again.

When I was brought back up, I spat my thank you *as soon as I drew my first breath.*

"For what?" Sabine said.

When I didn't have an immediate answer, she ordered Richard to dunk me, and under I went.

It went on forever. Eventually, because I was pathetic, I thanked them for cleaning my stink. I parroted whatever humiliating phrases that were hilarious to their juvenile minds. Finally, I stopped fighting, and they lost interest, abandoning me in the too-deep water to try and get back to shore.

Despite the heat of the summer, I couldn't stop shaking, a bone-deep chill following me into a dreamless sleep.

I had been so, so alone.

"Oh yes, yes, yes! Harder, fuck me like you mean it," Sabine ordered.

Sabine's cries thrusted me out of my memories. The slap of skin on skin ricocheted throughout the forest.

Richard and Sabine? *Gag.*

Richard's grunts punctuated each thrust. I was glad I was pressed against the tree and unable to see them. Of course, my shifter hearing allowed me to hear far, far too much. The gasps. Sabine's orders to go harder and stop being a weak bitch. It was less dirty talk and more contempt. Especially when Richard informed her that he was about to spend and she just about screeched in horror at the thought of him soiling her.

Moon, if Hell had a suggestion box, I'd be popping this scene into it because there was no worse torture I could think of.

Eventually, the two finished—it wasn't exactly that long since, despite the supernatural shifter stamina, Richard didn't seem to have all that much endurance.

Leave, I silently urged them. The sun was nearly set, and I still needed to get to the camp.

A slash of water, someone rinsing. Sabine's voice cut through, filling me in a moment later.

"You better spend at least twenty minutes in that river. I don't need you parading around with my scent over you like a prize."

"I'll dance with you at the party tonight?" Richard asked.

"Don't count on it."

With that, she left. Great. I hoped Richard would take that to be an exaggeration, but he tended to follow Sabine's orders to the letter.

Apparently, Sabine really didn't want anyone to know they were together, staggering their departures and washing off each other's scents. She'd always had her eyes on Jett. What were the odds that had changed? It surprised me only slightly that she'd jeopardize that by fooling around with Richard. It was clear it was hardly a passionate affair. She probably got off more on the fact she could boss him around than anything else.

Still, a party might be a stroke of luck if it was tonight. It was possible—shifters liked night affairs, after all. If it was just starting to get dark in the winter, it could be as early as six. I had no idea what the occasion was, but if Richard was there, there was a chance Jett and his family would at least show up. That could be my chance to get in the house.

Richard washed with excruciating thoroughness. I heard him splash in the water for ages. Seriously, wasn't he cold in there? It was frigid, with the sun having set.

Every minute was delaying me from rescuing Daphne. I didn't have a way to track the time, but he spent ages futzing around. Was he trying to air dry?

I held as still as possible, waiting. In the silence of night, my heartbeat felt too loud. Every minute was an eternity.

Then the worst possible urge struck me.

I had to sneeze. It was freezing out, and a cold wind had sent a chill right down my neck.

I tried to fight it, but the reflex hit me quickly. I clamped my hands over my mouth, biting down on my tongue as hard as possible.

The sound that released wasn't much more than a loud exhale.

Don't let him hear, don't let him hear.

But Richard, for all his brawn and lack of brains, had shifter hearing.

"Who the fuck is there?"

CHAPTER VII

I KEPT SILENT, HOPING he'd walk away and decide it was nothing.

Richard, unfortunately, was nothing if not stubborn.

"I said, who's there? I know you're over there."

He won't cross into Wind-Blood territory if he has half a brain, I assured myself.

But Richard wasn't the brightest.

And for all his faults, he had a very, very good sense of smell.

I held my breath, hoping he'd lose interest, but he wandered deeper into Wind-Blood territory. I was on the edge, just a few dozen feet from the water. *Where were Xander and his murderous patrol when you needed him?* Here was an *actual* intruder.

His footsteps drew closer. He didn't know exactly where I was, but that one muffled sneeze had been enough to give him a rough idea.

The footsteps stopped.

I couldn't look down without giving myself away, but they were dangerously close.

"What are you, hiding in the tree like some kind of squirrel?" he taunted.

Shit, he was right under the tree. Even closer than I'd feared.

"I know you're up there. Spying on me?" he growled. "You know what Moon-Ghost does to spies?"

There was a thud. The tree shook.

He'd just punched a freaking tree.

He might not be bright, but he was *strong*.

"If you're too scared to come down and fight me like a man, I'll drag you down myself," he yelled.

And then he began to climb.

Crap.

I stood up and looked around. Unfortunately, the other trees were too far to jump to with any accuracy. The scratch of hands came faster and faster as he climbed. My heart pounded at a dangerous pace. I was a decent bit up, but trees weren't exactly impossible to scale when you could dig your claws in.

I was out of time. I could move to the edge of the branch, but I doubted it would hold me. I'd need to jump and run.

Could I do it without being seen, though? My cursed red hair would make me a target. No one would want the Alpha Heir's fated mate to be back from the dead.

His scent permeated the top layer of the tree, wet and angry. I pressed myself close to the trunk as he climbed.

His head reached the level of my branch. Caught.

His nostrils flared as he saw me, bushy brows coming together in an expression that forgot to be angry for the sake of confusion. "You!"

I did the only thing I could.

I kicked him square in the face.

It was a good kick too. Over a decade of aggression behind it.

Richard lost his grip and fell back. I also fell backward, dropping to swing on the branch with my hands and jump down from the tree. *Which way to go?* Running into Wind-Blood would get me back where I started, and Richard would be able to go back and warn the others. Into Moon-Ghost was risky, but if he and Sabine came out, the area was probably deserted. I didn't have time to weigh my options.

I bolted for the river.

I didn't make it.

Richard recovered quickly from the kick to the head and was on my tail. He tackled me. The two of us grappled on the ground. He was naked, which would've grossed me out if I wasn't fighting for my life.

"How are you alive?" he snarled.

I didn't waste my breath answering. I clawed at his eyes.

"Omega bitch!" he howled.

I used the moment his grip loosened to kick away. He had a hundred pounds of muscle on me in human form. I didn't stand a chance.

Unless I shifted.

All the times they tormented me because I was weak, scrawny, pathetic.

Now I was a predator.

By the time he stood, I was on four legs, baring my fangs at him.

"Oh, the Omega puppy thinks she can fight." He belly laughed.

The honorable thing would be to wait for him to shift.

They'd never shown me a shred of honor, and it was a luxury I couldn't afford. Not with Daphne's safety on the line.

I surged towards Richard. The best defense was a good offense. Cole had taught me that.

I clamped my jaws on Richard's shoulder and tore.

With Xander and his patrol, I hadn't really wanted to hurt them.

I had no such issue when Richard's blood coated my tongue.

He roared in pain and shifted. There was no mockery now, only a bloodthirsty anger as he charged back. His wolf was larger than mine, but I was faster. And I'd learned to fight from someone stronger than us both.

Richard attacked with his size, but he was clumsy. I maneuvered around his advances, tearing at him with my teeth.

We edged closer to the water. He thought he was cornering

me, but I no longer felt entirely out of control. A strange calm took over me. It was like I could sense his movements before they happened, the way he leaned, the way he inhaled before charging. *Anticipate, counter.*

It was a violent brawl, but I was more than a victim.

I was hurting him, but it wasn't slowing him down.

My back paws sank into the wet dirt next to the river. I was at the edge.

Just like the Leo demon. I stopped attacking as much, shifting on my legs, slowing down.

Take the bait, Richard.

And in one final maneuver, Richard charged at me.

I couldn't move aside but instead dropped low. He sailed over me into the water.

Crack!

I turned around. Blood coated the rock in the water, his body limp next to it. Passed out.

The water threatened to carry him away.

I should let him drown.

It would be safer for me. And a vicious part felt it would be justice for everything he'd done to me, least of all his own attempts at drowning me.

He deserves it. The thought was a tantalizing whisper. It sounded like Cole.

Which is why I hated that I found myself heading into the water and dragging the wolf ashore. It was dangerous and foolish.

I hope this doesn't bite me in the ass, I thought, half-furious at myself.

I left him on the Wind-Blood side, praying Xander might choose to stray this way and capture a proper intruder. I shifted back to my human form and crossed the river, hissing in pain. I'd agitated everything I'd managed to heal earlier.

I was naked, again. My clothes were in shreds.

But Richard had already been naked...

My eyes seized on a discarded pile of clothing.

It was gross. I didn't want to wear his dirty clothing, which was too big for me and stank like enemies. But it would help mask my scent.

Daphne better appreciate this.

CHAPTER VIII

I T TOOK HOURS TO reach the edge of town. I moved quietly in the shadows, stretching my hearing as best I could to listen for anyone coming near.

I couldn't afford to get caught.

I may have spent months in Hell, but my old territory was familiar under my feet. Unlike the Wind-Blood territory, I knew every tree and rock in Moon-Ghost. I'd certainly spent enough time hiding in all the hidden sanctuaries the territory possessed.

Richard's foul stench covered me. I'd ripped off the bottom of his pant legs and shirts, using the fabric to tie back my hair and obscure the distinct red color.

They'd discussed a party. Pack events weren't exactly uncommon, but when I'd lived here, I'd avoided each and every one like it was a brand of torture.

The thrum of music announced this party was well underway. The bass pounded through the ground. It actually was somewhat unpleasant with my shifter hearing, but others must've been used to it.

There was no time for hesitation. The Kings's house was on the opposite side of camp. I could either walk around or through. Around would be slower and might draw the suspicions of anyone enjoying some time on the fringe.

That left cutting straight through as my only real option.

I refused to let myself embrace the fear that threatened to overwhelm me.

I moved into the crowd.

I couldn't walk so fast that I drew attention or stall long enough for people to stare. It was close to midnight, and the party had clearly started a while ago. It had taken forever, walking in my human form so as to not rip up Richard's clothing or draw attention from any patrols. Sabine had no doubt been back in a fraction of the time.

My entrance went unnoticed. Everyone was out tonight, and it seemed every shifter from teenage years on was getting sloshed.

"Happy birthday to the Alpha Heir!" someone called as a salute before downing the contents of their plastic cup.

His birthday. I knew it, of course—February 17th. It was basically a pack holiday.

That settled the mystery of the occasion. Which was good—surely Jett's parents would be out of the house at the party.

It was just a week after my own. I was a year older now too.

I frowned. Was I? Or had dying stopped the aging process?

I still had so many freaking questions. All over again, I resent-
ed Cole and his insistence on secret keeping. If I ever saw him
again, I was going to demand answers, even if he was furious
at me.

Of course, now that I'd come back to the realm of the
living, there was no reason to think I'd wind back up in Hell. I
might never see the grumpy Alpha ever again. Might just take
Daphne and flee to the edges of the continent.

"Watch where you're going," someone growled, bumping
into me.

I mumbled an apology under my breath, my heart shoved
into my throat as I braced for discovery.

But the male who'd knocked into me kept going, uninter-
ested. My hair coverings were working well enough, and even
though I wasn't exactly party ready, I was blending.

There was no time to waste. I made my way farther in,
constantly scanning the crowd for my old tormentors.

Call it an old survival mechanism, but I was attuned to the
presence of my old bullies.

It was Sabine I first laid eyes on.

I spotted her in my periphery, refusing to fully turn my
neck and see. She was at the center of the crowd, dancing on
a car hood.

For a moment, anger threatened to overtake me. The raw
fury I felt took me off guard. It wasn't like what I'd felt for
Richard. I despised him, but he was a tool.

Sabine? The bitch had killed me.

It went a little deeper than despise.

And when I saw her drag another shifter in front, leering down at a younger girl, barely a teenager, while her goons held her in place?

I was furious.

The girl must've been a replacement Omega. The urge to claw Sabine's face off was overwhelming. I might even be able to win. My hands tingled, and I clenched them into fists to tamp down on any green sparks that might give me away.

I wanted to go over there and fight Sabine so badly. Give her a taste of her own medicine. The desire for retribution warmed my very blood.

But even if I could win, I'd blow my cover. All my hard work would be for nothing because, while I might be able to win against Sabine, I had no chance in a hundred-on-one fight.

I forced myself to turn away from the young shifter, who would be in for a long night of torment.

I hated myself more than a little in that moment.

The rest of the journey to the Kings's house was uninterrupted. Everyone was caught up in the revelry. The Alphas ran the pack, and they passed it down from father to son. Maddox might rule us now, but one day, when he stepped down or died, Jett would take over.

I had doubts about Maddox King's willingness to relinquish power, though.

But even being the Alpha Heir was enough to warrant an annual celebration. People were drunk and cheerful. I kept my head down, my hair coverings in place.

And then I was in front of the house.

Of course, I wasn't stupid enough to go right in the front door. Even half-drunk, pack sentinels would be watching around for mischief. Instead, I wandered around the side. The King residence was completely unlike the humble cabins of the Wind-Blood territory. It was funny. There, the Alpha's home looked the same as any other.

This was a mansion.

I wasn't an expert on the layout, having never been inside. When I was alive, I'd made it my mission to avoid the place at all costs.

But I couldn't afford to stay out, exposed. I went around back, tasting the air to detect anyone nearby and coming up empty.

The house was elevated, the windows about six feet off the ground. I jumped and pulled myself just up to the sill to look inside. It was the kitchen, which, thankfully, was deserted. No lights were on, which hopefully meant nobody was home.

With any luck, no one would be running in for supplies. Everything was almost certainly sourced from the dining hall anyway, instead of the Alpha's personal residence. I'd hoped for a bathroom or something more concealed, but this would have to do.

Now to get in.

Breaking a window would be loud. I hoisted myself up, carefully balancing on the windowsill, and eased the window up. Unlocked.

But of course it was unlocked. No one was suicidal enough to sneak into Maddox King's home.

Good thing I'm already dead.

I didn't pause to question my good fortune. Instead, I eased the window back down once inside and moved as quickly as I could to hide in the shadows. No matter how I strained my hearing, the house seemed silent, but it was hard to be sure with the steady thrum of bass outside polluting the silence.

Finding the cells was my next challenge. I expected to feel anxious, moving so deeply in the territory of my enemy. Breathing in the scent of my fated mate, who forsook me. My heart should've been pounding.

Yet, none of that happened. Jett's lingering scent did nothing but irritate me. An unnatural calm took over as I searched the house. The stairs to the basement were easy enough to find. A finished space, built like a space for the King family to relax.

The cells, as it turned out, were another layer beyond that.

There was no mistaking the door to the dungeon. While the rest of the King residence was a manicured mansion fit for hosting and curated appeal, there was no masking the scents that leaked out of the door. Dirt. Blood. Despair.

I bit down on the growl in my throat at the thought of Daphne's own despair mixing in with that.

The door opened to a rickety old set of stairs. I climbed down them, two at a time, while keeping my movement quiet.

I'd seen a glimpse of the cells in my scrying, but I was utterly unprepared for what I found.

What lay under Maddox's house reminded me more of the dungeon in Cole's castle than the pristine mansion I'd walked through above. Rows and rows of cells. The distasteful feel of silver crawled over my skin. Not as bad as when I'd stepped in the room with that box, but still unpleasant.

The cells were unguarded and, as best I could tell, empty. I stalked through, checking each one.

Am I too late? My search grew more frantic. *No. She has to be here.*

Then, there. At the very end of the row of cells, I spotted her. Her true scent was buried under grime and dirt, but I peeled back the layers in my head and tasted her. My friend.

"Daphne," I rasped. Her name was a plea. Please be okay.

She jerked as if struck, then twisted her body, the tattered blanket that had covered her falling back as she turned.

Her eyes snapped wide in recognition as she saw me.

"Avery!"

CHAPTER IX

"Shhh," I said quickly, glancing back to the front of the room. I hadn't shut the door fully behind me, terrified it might lock automatically.

"Avery, is it really you?" Her voice was quieter, but there was raw shock in her eyes.

I nodded in confirmation. "It's me."

"How? I thought... Sabine said they'd killed you."

Sabine had told the truth, but I didn't want to get into that right now. I might have adjusted to the fact I'd died and gone to Hell, but that was kind of a lot to take in. "I'll explain later. I'm getting you out of here."

Daphne stood upright, swaying on her feet. I took in her appearance, my lips twisting back as my fangs threatened to come forth.

How dare they?

Her clothes were in tatters, nothing more than a thin tee and jeans that had previously been fashionably ripped and hugged her curves. Now, they were just torn and threatened to fall off of her. She'd lost weight, her collarbones in sharp relief. Her once muscular frame was nearly as skinny as mine. Her lustrous hair was matted with dark patches of caked blood.

She hadn't just been shoved down here. They'd *hurt* her.

They'd hurt my best friend, and I would kill them all for it.

"Um, Avery? What's happening to your eyes?"

Her words startled me out of my thoughts. I shook my head, hoping to clear away whatever had happened. "Sorry." I switched my attention to the cell. Long silver poles with a giant lock shutting the door closed her in. "Do you know where the keys are?"

If possible, Daphne wilted. "Maddox always keeps them on him."

Crap. I looked around for any type of wire or stick in hopes I could pick the lock but came up empty.

I also didn't know how to pick locks.

In desperation, I grabbed for the bars.

"Don't!" Daphne warned, seeing my movement.

It was too late. I knew it would hurt, but I hadn't been entirely braced for how badly. Sticking my hands into a live flame would've hurt less. I bit on my tongue so hard it bled to stop from crying out.

"The metal burns. It's not natural."

"It's silver," I explained. But Cole had said if I was in true balance with my wolf, I could bend silver like any other metal.

I took a breath and tried again.

Nothing. Nothing but blistering pain.

Daphne casted a worried look towards the way I'd come.

"Avery, you have to go. Just leave me here."

"Never," I vowed.

"Listen to me! They won't kill me because of my father. But you're not safe here. If they find out you're alive…"

Her warning was cut off as the door creaked open. Both of us frozen in place. The sound was quiet, barely there.

A death knell.

Footsteps thundered in a slow, measured pace down the stairs. One, then another. I looked around frantically for a place to hide and came up empty.

"Someone's sneaking into my dungeon," a low, deadly voice called out.

Maddox.

Step.

Step.

"Someone's going to *pay*."

Step.

Step.

Then he was at the bottom of the stairs. Looking straight at me.

"What do we have here?" He continued his unhurried march toward me. His nostrils flared in recognition when he placed me. "You."

"Sorry, is this not where the birthday party is?" I asked,

stepping forward. I nearly peed myself taking a step towards Maddox, the terrifying wolf I'd spent my childhood hiding from. But he wasn't going to get through Daphne without going through me first. "The invite didn't say."

"I should've put you down when you were born."

I scoffed. "Is that any way to treat your son's moon-matched mate?" I almost choked on the title, only managing because I knew it would piss him off. And if I wanted to stand a chance against the Moon-Ghost Alpha, who had been in charge longer than I'd been alive, I would need him to be a little off his gear.

"You didn't deserve the honor," Maddox growled, my words having the desired effect.

I didn't ask to be his goddess-damned mate! "You could've just let me leave. There was no need to kill me for being an unworthy mate," I said with an eye roll, acting deliberately blasé while I looked him over.

He threw his head back and laughed. It was a dark sound.

The movement revealed a glint of metal hanging on his belt. *The keys.*

"But I'll fix that now," he assured me when the laughter died. "And once you're properly in the ground, I'm going to kill that disloyal bitch for conspiring with you."

That was all the warning Maddox gave before charging.

Maddox was big, easily over six feet, and solid muscle. And while he may have been in his seventies, it only meant he'd grown in strength.

Sparring with Cole was sometimes a dance, a game of chess, at high speed.

Maddox was a fight for survival.

On his initial charge, he nearly grasped his hands around my throat. I managed to duck away, but I didn't stand much of a chance.

He'd been fighting bloody battles for decades. He was bigger and stronger than Richard, but he wasn't a simple opponent that I could outmaneuver like Richard had been.

We went back and forth, attack, counter. I landed a solid kick, but Maddox grabbed my leg before I could retract. His reflexes were fast.

Faster than mine.

He flung me across the hallway.

I sailed over forty feet before crashing against the stone wall. I screamed in pain, the tender flesh on my sides ripping open.

But I couldn't let that slow me. In the few seconds it took me to get to my feet and start towards him, he'd unlocked the cell and gripped Daphne in his arms, clawed hand under her throat.

"Submit and I'll deal with you first. Otherwise, I'm going to spray your pretty friend's throat on the wall."

He was over twenty feet away.

I didn't think. Instinct took over.

Green lighting exploded out of my palms, landing a direct hit on his arm. He jerked back, loosening enough that Daphne was able to get out of his grip, even in her weakened state. I didn't hesitate to charge.

"Unnatural bitch," Maddox growled.

"Run," I ordered Daphne, charging against the Alpha. I tried to summon the sparks again, but little came. We grappled. I went for every low blow I could, gouging his eyes, biting his fingers, groin shots. It wasn't pretty, but Maddox was ruthless in return. He punched my kidneys hard enough to make me stumble back and landed a blow to my head that had me spewing blood.

And then his hands were wrapped around my throat.

He thrust me against a cell, the silver digging into my back, burning.

"I'm going to enjoy watching the life bleed out of you," he said, his grip tightening slowly like he was savoring it.

My vision turned spotty.

I prayed Daphne was using the time to run. I'd planned on us escaping together, but there was no way I could survive this.

It was funny, that moment before death. It could only have been a second, maybe two, but in it, Cole's face flashed a hundred times in my blurring vision.

I'm sorry, Cole. I wasn't sure what for. Betraying him? The fact he'd kept secrets from me? Or simply the fact I'd never see him again?

Maddox's grip was suffocating. I gasped, trying and failing to draw the oxygen in.

"Fight, Avery!" Daphne called.

She hadn't run.

"And once you're dead, I'm *really* going to have my fun with her," Maddox gloated.

No.

The thought wasn't a word.

It was an explosion.

My hands were limp by my sides, but light exploded out of me. Not sparks, not lightning, but a burst of green that threw Maddox back off of me.

It wasn't like when he threw me against the wall. It was a flash and then he crashed against the wall, collapsing down onto the floor, his head cut open as blood spilled out.

The hallway was silent. He wasn't breathing.

Daphne was by my side in a second, checking me over even though she could barely stand.

"Is he dead?" She cast a terrified glance toward me.

"I suppose I should thank you for that."

The words didn't come from me.

No.

They came from my fated mate, my bully, my tormentor of more than a decade.

Jett King stood at the base of the stairs, murder in his eyes.

"In the end, you weren't entirely useless as a moon-matched mate." He was immaculate, a younger version of his father, lean muscle, chiseled jaw, a sardonic twist of his lips as he took in the scene. "As thanks, I think I'll kill you both."

I tried to summon the green light again, but whatever power I'd had, I was tapped out. My vision was still half gone from Maddox's choke hold. Daphne tried to stand in front of me, but she was only marginally better off than I was.

Jett looked to be in perfect condition.

There was no way I was going to survive him.

"Avery!"

Cole.

It was impossible, but there, behind me, was a portal of swirling light, Cole in the center.

Jett spotted him too. "What that fuck is that?"

Cole's attention shifted from me to the Alpha Heir.

"So he's the one." Cole didn't wear his anger as easily as Maddox or Jett. Instead, it was the subtle twitch of his jaw that told me Jett was marked for death.

Jett was too brave or too stupid to note the threat. He started towards us to make good on his promises.

"Step through the portal, now!" Cole snapped.

Jett charged at us, but desperation made me faster, even through the pain.

I didn't hesitate.

In one leap, I grabbed Daphne and jumped through.

CHAPTER X

F ALLING THROUGH THE PORTAL back to the land of the living was one of the most absolutely unpleasant sensations I'd ever experienced—and I say this as someone who was literally killed.

The second time through returning to the land of the dead was only a mild improvement.

Pure momentum pushed us through. My head felt like it was tossed in a blender, my brain spinning round and round and round. I twisted onto my side in time to watch the portal flicker shut with a furious Jett still running towards it.

I knew on instinct we hadn't returned to the castle I'd spent the past few months living in. A glance around confirmed it. That castle had been black, barren rock that glistened in dim torchlight and was borderline freezing.

This castle felt more like a palace. Better lit, taller ceilings, and a plush red carpet that had eased the landing.

Daphne twitched, her body over mine. I'd broken our fall after dragging us through.

My dazed examination fell aside as I checked on my best

friend. My hands pressed all over her body, checking to make sure she was in one piece.

"I should be doing that to you," she said with a whimper. "I think I'm gonna hurl."

I opened my mouth to reassure her when she just disappeared.

One second, there, on top of me. The next, she was gone. I flicked my gaze up and there was Cole, staring down with an expression I couldn't decipher. It didn't feel overly welcoming.

"What did you just do with my friend?" I demanded.

"She's being seen by healers," he said, dismissing me.

"You can't just do that!" I got to my feet, brushing invisible dirt off the pants I'd stolen from Richard.

"I can't?" Suddenly Cole was right in my face, the distance between us swallowed in a fraction of a second. "I'll do anything I godsdamn please. You broke out of Hell, killed a living shifter, and nearly got yourself sent to Tartarus in the process."

"So?" My best friend needed me. That was all that mattered.

"You're the most reckless woman in all the realms. You have *no* idea about the danger you put yourself in."

The fury in his words, laced with concern, took me aback.

It was a half-step stumble that had me against a wall. The fraction of a movement only urged Cole on, ready to give chase.

"You poisoned me with your kiss."

"I did what I had to do," I said, defiant. In another time, I might've felt bad, but I'd done it all to rescue Daphne. Who he'd *poofed* away before I could even properly check on her.

"Then I'll do what I have to." A threat. A promise. "Starting with replacing the taste of the poison you left on my lips."

That was all the warning he gave before his mouth crashed into mine. He claimed my lips, devouring me. It was an angry kiss, a furious, vengeful one that threatened to sap the last remaining strength I possessed. My blood flavored the violent kiss, drenching us both. His hand rested on my throat, claiming the space Maddox had threatened to suffocate me with moments ago. The adrenaline of the fighting spurred me on.

He tasted better than I'd allowed myself to remember. Like smoke and death and a dark, dark promise. It was nectar on my tongue.

I thought I'd never taste him again. The idea was too unbearable to contemplate.

His spare hand went to my shirt. I was half drunk on the kiss, barely processing until I heard the sound of fabric ripping.

My eyes widened. Cole's amber ones met them, glowing with fury. "You *reek* of another male."

I should've stopped him. Should've protested that I wasn't going to get naked in front of him.

But I *did* reek of Richard's scent, and I was exhausted and had nearly died, *again*, and I would've much preferred to smell like Cole.

The shirt fell to the floor in tatters.

Then his lips were against mine again. I clawed at his shirt in turn, dragging my nails down his back as I pulled the silky fabric away. It was the same fine material he often wore, and as decadent as the sensation of my fingers over silk was, I wanted to feel him against me. It was instinct. It was animalistic. There was little awareness of our actions beyond a need to have him all over me.

He pushed harder, losing the restraint that held him back. I hadn't even realized he was holding back until he slipped, but that was what Cole was. A storm of power in a carefully placed net.

I groaned, and the source was both pain and pleasure. Pleasure because Cole was here. Whatever our differences, he was touching me and it made my blood hum.

But also because the stone was digging into my back and I was pretty sure I had a bit of internal bleeding going on. It was probably shock that had kept me from feeling the depth of that realization. It didn't hurt quite as much as it should, but it was starting to as the adrenaline of the battle wore off.

Cole pulled back with a foul curse.

"You're hurt."

I walked away from a fight with the Moon-Ghost Alpha. It'd be weird if I wasn't. "I won."

Cole towered over me, his gaze firm as he tilted my chin back with two fingers, as if I needed any encouragement to look at him. "You did."

I sagged slightly, the acknowledgment making me weak.

Or the blood loss. That was also a possibility.

Cole caught me before I could fall. I was in his arms in an instant, tucked against him like I hadn't poisoned him a few days ago.

"Where are we going?" My voice was thready.

"You need healing."

"You're not just going to *poof* me away too?" Sexy-as-heck kiss or not, I wasn't going to forgive him for taking Daphne away when I'd only just gotten her back. I trusted Cole in this, even if I was stunned he'd been able to do that, but I was still annoyed.

He chuckled. "You'll have to settle for me carrying you."

That was the issue with Cole.

It was too easy to settle for any scrap he'd give me. I was so lonely I'd take them all and smother myself with them.

CHAPTER XI

COLE CARRIED ME, AND while I fought to stay awake in his arms, sleep threatened to claim me at any given moment. He strode through hallways with the same confidence he always moved with.

In the back of my mind, I knew this was it. We were going to finally need to confront those things he'd told me. The fact he was the King of Hell, for one.

That I'd been his queen.

I meant to bring it up, I did. But then he took me to a room and placed me down on a bed. I sank into the mattress, immediately comforted, curling in.

And then I knew nothing.

My sleep was black. At moments, I edged towards awareness. There were voices. Growling. A gruff, grumpy voice that barked demands. A familiar female one that never changed. Warmth. My body stitched back together. Aches that had become familiar went away.

I woke up slowly. My eyes fluttered open, the rest of my body heavy.

I was in a magnificent room. A wave of déjà vu hit me from the time I'd woken up in Hecate's guest room after being petrified. But this room was a thousand times more decadent. It was the size of a small house, if the bits of it I saw while lying down were any indication. Large curtains hung floor to ceiling on the far wall. The bedposts spiraled up at least eight feet, steady beams that were ornately carved. The rest of the furniture I could make out to one side was similarly spectacular.

My examination of the room ended when I saw Cole asleep, upright in the chair next to the bed.

It was the second time I'd ever seen Cole asleep. And the only time not at my own hand.

His face lost the harsh, controlled tilt I was accustomed to. Even when he flirted or teased me, there was an element of restraint that never escaped him. But here, the curls of his black hair fell aside. His head was tilted back, throat exposed. Skin trailed down, his shirt only half-buttoned with the edges of that entrancing tattoo peeking out.

"Developing a penchant for voyeurism?"

I jolted, flicking up to see Cole's eyes open in narrow slits as his lip curled into a familiar twist.

My cheeks heated. "Just wondering how many hours I slept that you fell asleep waiting for me to wake up."

A beat, and I knew more time had passed than I'd realized.

"It's been four days." The words were said without a trace

of humor.

I started to sit up. *Four days?* "I need to get to Daphne—"

He was out of the chair in half a heartbeat, and with one hand, pushed me back down. "Your friend is fine. You'll rest more until Hecate is confident you're well."

Annoyance flared. "*I'm fine.* Let me go to my friend."

Cole's face said he wouldn't be yielding, but I attempted to sit up again anyway.

The blanket started to fall away, and another awareness took over.

I blinked. My clothes—all of them—were missing. "Where the frick are my clothes?"

His amber eyes narrowed on me, drinking in the exposed skin in a way that made me want to bare my chest instead of cover it.

I dragged the blanket up.

"I won't have you in my bed wearing another male's clothing. You'll wear my scent or nothing at all."

His words appealed to a dark part of me more than I cared to admit. They sent a stir all the way down my spine to my core.

But I was a bit tired of waking up without clothing. "Who's the pervert now?" I snarked.

"*I* never denied it. Not when it comes to you."

I couldn't say anything to that, so I changed back to the original subject.

"Just get me some clothing so I can go see Daphne—"

That was as far as I got before something snapped in Cole.

One moment, he was in the chair beside me.

By the time I drew my next breath, he was on top of me. The plush blankets were the only barrier between us, but somehow they didn't feel like much protection.

The bed sank under his weight. His thighs pushed in on my hips, holding me down, while his hands fell on either side of the pillow my head rested on.

His face was my entire world at this distance. His scent was familiar and delicious and I wanted to wrap myself in it.

"You haven't eaten in at least a week. You haven't slept—just passed out when the adrenaline faded. Your body was half torn apart when you stumbled through the portal. I barely got to you in time, thanks to your little stunt with the moonstone. I'm so furious with you that I can barely speak, but I can't even yell at you properly until I'm confident you won't immediately stumble onto another suicidal mission."

I cringed slightly at his harsh tone. Gone was the light flirtation of moments ago.

"You will stay in this bed until I declare otherwise. If you even *attempt* to get out before you're completely healed, I will personally tie you to this bed and keep you here for a month."

"That's going to be kind of inconvenient unless you want me peeing in the sheets." I deflected with humor because Cole was far, far too close for me to think straight. It was a bluff, though. If I'd been out for four days, then I hadn't had a sip of water in almost a week. I was tapped out, but surely he'd see how unreasonable he was being, right?

Cole growled, a deep, animalistic sound that said his wolf was a hairsbreadth from the surface. That was likely a "no" on reasonable then.

"I'll carry you to the damn toilet if I have to, but you're not leaving this room until I say so."

"Fine." The fight slipped out of me. The truth was, I was exhausted. I may have rested for days, but just this little interaction drained me. "I'm too tired to argue."

He huffed. "That would be a first, and it's even more of a sign I'm right if you're admitting it."

I frowned. "Is that your way of calling me stubborn?"

His lips quirked up, the fury seeming to dissipate now that I wasn't attempting to get out of bed. "Little wolf, I have a hundred different ways to describe your moods."

I rolled my eyes. None of them flattering, of that I was sure.

I settled back into the covers, Cole still leaning over me.

"Are you going to stay there the entire time?"

He was still perched over me, his presence bearing down on me in a way that was simultaneously comforting and threatening.

"I'm quite tempted." He didn't say it in a teasing tone, but rather a contemplative one. "Sometimes, I think if I so much as blink, I might lose you again." But a moment later, he eased off. Instead of heading off the bed back to the chair, he stayed in the bed.

It was massive, I reasoned. But he wasn't exactly making any grand effort to put some real space between us.

And his scent was a comfort I had missed more than I had realized.

Probably was convinced I'd try to slip out again at any moment. At this point, I knew Cole well enough not to test him on his threat to tie me to the bed.

"Is Daphne okay?" I asked.

"Your friend is being taken care of. She's doing better than you, I'd say." He sounded almost accusatory, like it was her fault I'd come back all beat up.

"They kept her in a cage of silver," I hissed in her defense.

He was at once soothing, fingers trailing through my hair, petting me in slow, rhythmic motions that eased my fury. "You rescued her. She'll be fine, little wolf. She's under my protection. No one will touch her. Just sleep for now."

In this, again, I trusted him.

"You didn't show up in my dreams this time," I said as my eyes shut. That, maybe more than anything, I needed answers on. I was too tired to pry them from him now, a task that was borderline impossible under the best of circumstances.

He snorted softly. "If you'd actually been sleeping, perhaps. It's not so easy when you're completely passed out."

"Excuses." The word came out as a huff and turned into a

yawn.

"Then find me in your dreams if you wish to see me."

CHAPTER XII

*W*E WERE IN THE *same castle I currently rested in. Of that, I was strangely certain. It made the dream an abnormality.*

"My dreams don't normally have man-made objects in them," I mused aloud.

"The bed was just an exception then?" Cole asked, startling me.

I don't know why I was surprised he was there. He'd starred in every dream I had, even though he'd just been a disembodied voice.

I chose to ignore his reference to the one dream I'd had of him, where he'd been very corporeal. I hadn't known it was actually Cole. Which meant I'd given into my every desire and enjoyed the dream thoroughly.

It'd be a happy memory if not for the mortification that Cole had actually seen me begging to come under his tongue.

"Are you going to finally explain why you're in my dreams?" I demanded, changing the subject. "Or are you going to keep more secrets?"

Cole's lip quirked up. "You were more fun when you didn't realize it was actually me."

I growled. "Wonder why that is."

"Because you didn't feel the need to pretend to hold back every lustful thought that crossed your mind?" the male guessed, as if it had been a real question.

My cheeks turned the same red as my hair, even my dream self was unsafe from my blushes. I turned away from Cole and explored the surroundings. Normally, we were in some outdoor setting. Now, we were atop the castle. On top of a tower, it seemed, by the small space. I wedged myself in one of the embrasures and sat, looking out. I could see the entire capital city from here, solidifying where I was. But unlike when I'd found the place earlier, it was utterly deserted.

"Can you just give me answers?" I pleaded. "I can't take much more of this, Cole. I'm sick of not knowing."

Cole moved to the merlon, leaning over with his arms folded. I glanced up at him. His expression turned contemplative.

"The first time I found you in your dreams, you caught me off guard."

"You were there—physically, I mean." It had been when I was just a kid, stuffed in a locker and passed out.

He nodded. "I hid after that. I didn't want to interact with you."

I winced, the words an unexpected blow. For ages, the voice I'd thought had been my subconscious had been my one true confidant, where I'd let myself feel the worst of the rejection of my pack that I hid from even Daphne. And I'd just been a burden to Cole?

"But I couldn't stay away," Cole continued. "I told myself I'd hide in your dreams, just check up on you."

"But you spoke to me."

"It was impossible to resist," he said with a shake of his head.

"But how?" I asked. "How was any of this possible? You said... you said I was your queen. Did we know each other? How was that possible?"

I sensed Cole tense rather than saw it. I expected him to clam up, but apparently, Cole was in an uncharacteristically sharing mood. Maybe he'd finally realized all the secrets had a way of backfiring. "I shouldn't have told you that."

Or not.

"But you did," I insisted. "You can't unring that bell, Cole. I have a right to know." I wasn't going to be kept in the dark again.

"And I have a right to lock you up and make sure you never move an inch without my knowing," Cole growled.

I resisted the urge to point out he'd already threatened to do that and was only holding back because I was currently obediently sleeping.

"Can't you give me any answers?" I pushed.

The silence was endless.

"You were my queen, and it left us with a link."

I opened my mouth to ask a hundred more questions, but he cut me off with a sigh that was so uncharacteristic I had to glance up and see if he'd somehow aged eighty years.

"Don't make me say more than that, Avery. Spare me that cruelty."

And then the dream was over.

I rolled to the side. Cole was asleep, or had been, on the pillow next to me. His breathing shifted as his eyes flicked open.

We didn't talk about the dream. I wanted answers, but something in me ached at the thought of hurting him by making him explain. Whatever it was, it was clearly beyond painful for him to discuss.

That didn't mean I was going to give up on answers. No. It just meant I'd need to find someone else to give them to me.

If I thought one little nap was all it would take for Cole to let me out of bed, I was sorely mistaken. He didn't actually make good on his threat to carry me to the bathroom, but on the rare occasion I was allowed to leave the bed, he stayed close enough to make me blush.

His presence was constant. Food appeared in the room—he never left to request it or bring anything back. No one came to visit either. I eventually demanded he at least give me something to read, and a mountain of books was suddenly piled up next to the bed. It reminded me of the books I'd stolen from the library back in the previous castle. I kind of felt bad I'd never actually returned them to the library, but then again, it had just been me, Cole, and a hundred petrified creatures that had no use for the books.

We passed the time reading, often in companionable silence. Sometimes Cole sprawled out on the bed, propped up as he watched over me from the edge of a thick book, but he often took the chair next to the bed instead.

I liked it better when he was in the bed. But I never actually invited him up.

The dreams were present too. I wanted to avoid sleeping, to avoid seeing him there. It felt somehow even more intimate, and I was unable to confront the way I'd spoken to him for years in them. Each one took place in a different spot. Yet each was a location in Hell, of that I grew more certain. Always unique, but the red sky often followed us. If I wanted to be allowed to leave, I needed to rest. I'd had bruises on my neck after what Maddox did, which healed quickly but not fast enough for Cole's taste. He'd spent a lot of time staring at my throat until they healed. The rest of my injuries also healed, though no healer ever visited when I was awake.

It was over four days before Cole unleashed me on the palace.

CHAPTER XIII

*E**XIT LEFT, DOWN THE hall, then go down one floor and take the first right.*

Those were Cole's directions to find Daphne.

The morning he cleared me, I nearly took off in a sprint. I'd commandeered a shirt from Cole that fell to the middle of my thighs. Throughout the four days, he'd denied my requests for clothing, claiming to need to inspect the bruises as they healed on my sides. For all the healing I'd magically done after Xander ripped me apart, my fight with Maddox had wrecked my side again.

When I'd put the shirt on, I'd expected Cole to tease me. Maybe a comment that at least this time I'd asked before taking it.

Instead, he'd given me a look that said I might wind up back in bed for a very different reason.

The tension between us was palpable. Against my better judgment, I continued to lust after Cole. He had a body that made you think of sex, that made your toes curl, and a confidence that let you know he could deliver. The few times we'd tapped into that tension, the results had been explosive.

I mean, I wasn't exactly experienced. It could totally be the fact he was the only guy I'd kissed.

But I doubted that. I suspected even if I'd had sex with a hundred guys, Cole would still blow them all out of the water.

Too bad I had no intention of finding out.

My wolf wanted him too. In him, she saw a packmate. An Alpha, one she could respect, if not actually submit to. The days with him hovering around had her wanting to curl up in his bed and never leave.

Of course, my wolf tended to want to roll over and get belly rubs from the brute, so her judgment wasn't to be trusted. Whatever Cole said about us being one and the same, that was a clear divide.

No, I couldn't have Cole. Not in truth. There were too many secrets for me to trust him. I'd asked and asked, but he seemed no more willing to share any answers than before I'd left. He was the freaking King of Hell, and if someone didn't tell me what that really meant soon, I might go mad.

Later, I'd seek answers. Maybe Hecate would be willing to share more. She'd been the only one to give me any insight into the mess that was this world.

But first, I needed to see Daphne.

The castle I'd lived in before had been empty of anyone but Cole and one murderous snake-haired bitch. I'd expected the same (minus Medusa).

Clearly, that was incorrect.

The hallways were filled with people. The soundproofing of Cole's bedroom must've been impeccable because I'd never heard a thing. Yet now, I saw them. Staff, at least some of them, by the simple uniforms they wore. Others were in more ornate clothing decorated with jewelry. Some looked like me, human-shaped or similar, with slight modifications like animal tails or blue skin. Others were... different. I tried not to stare, especially since everyone seemed to be working very hard to not stare at *me*.

As I walked down the hallway, trying to not screw up the directions Cole had given me, it was impossible to miss their glances. The whispered comments behind hands. Of course, whispers were nothing I couldn't easily overhear.

"Is that her?" someone asked as I passed by.

"It has to be. I mean, that's definitely the king's shirt."

Apparently, black silk was a signature look of Cole's if they could tell at a glance. I refused to feel embarrassed, though I wished I'd taken a spare set of pants even if they stood no chance of fitting, not when Cole's legs were so much longer than mine. In that ensemble, I would've looked like a kid playing dress-up.

In just a shirt... it was a bit more *salacious*.

That would've explained away the whispers, except some seemed to go beyond that.

"She's back," someone said. I couldn't tell if it was horror or awe in their voice and didn't stop to ask.

What do they mean by back? I'd never met any of these people before.

I moved down the stairs two steps at a time after passing the endless hallway. When I reached the next floor, the wall on my right opened to a large open window. I halted my quest to get to Daphne and looked out.

With one look, I confirmed my suspicion.

This was the capital. The same place I'd looked out on in my dream with Cole, yet now it was filled with motion and sound. There was nothing beyond the general din of day-to-day life that reached up to the floor I was on, but the city was bustling. The market I'd found the strange cat in was by the entrance, as I remembered. Though I couldn't make out the specific bar I'd found the Libra demon at, there was clearly no shortage of restaurants and pubs and other stores.

Why did Cole keep this from me? It shouldn't have mattered, but he'd put such a line in the sand over taking me to the city. Yet now, as I looked out, I felt almost at home. Or if not at home, like this place could become one.

It was a ridiculous thought. I had no home. All that mattered was Daphne. I turned away from the window and continued down the hall to find my friend.

But the thought lingered anyway.

I rounded the corner and found an open door. The scent of healing herbs and fresh linens hit my nose first. A medical wing, clearly. Rows of beds lined the room, white fabric hugging them. And there was my best friend, sitting up in one of them.

"Daphne!" I couldn't contain my joy at seeing my friend. I darted over to the bedside, not even bothering to scan the room for other inhabitants.

My friend met my exuberance with an embrace.

"Avery! You're okay," she said, pulling back and looking me over. "They wouldn't tell me anything about you. But it looks like you healed."

"You look way better too." It was true. It had been a little over a week, but courtesy of whatever they had done in combination with her natural shifter resiliency, Daphne looked almost like the girl I remembered instead of the shell of herself I'd found in the Moon-Ghost cell.

At that moment, a rush of gratitude rose in my chest. Whatever issues I had with Cole, he'd kept my friend safe.

He'd also kept me from her, which I still didn't agree with, but she was okay. Better than okay.

Daphne pulled me down with her on the bed. It felt good to have my best friend back.

"Avery, where are we? Where have you been all these months?" She inhaled. "And why do you smell like a male?"

Despite the circumstances, Daphne gave me a girlish look, her brows wriggling in question.

I tugged at the collar of the shirt. "I have a lot to tell you."

It would've been easy to put the conversation off, but she deserved to know. Even if, as it became clear during my explanation, my answers left a lot to be desired. There were gaps as I told her about dying and winding up in Hell. She took it in stride. I told her an abridged version, describing my training with Cole. I skipped over less savory details, like him setting the demon on me in his training, just explaining he was "effective." I also skipped over the stuff about me having been his queen since I still didn't understand what that meant, only mentioning he seemed to be in charge here, although I'd never been here before. I did tell her I'd poisoned him to rescue her—skipping my particular methodology—and about my mysterious powers. She quizzed me on them, but unfortunately, I didn't understand how they worked.

"If I'm in Hell too," Daphne asked after she'd had a few minutes to process, "does that mean I'm also dead?"

"No more than Avery is now alive after having traipsed through a portal to rescue you."

I twisted to see who had interjected. A familiar face greeted me, beautiful and ethereal, as if the melodic voice could ever have been mistaken.

"Welcome back, *Soteria*. We have much to discuss."

CHAPTER XIV

"**H**ECATE!" I EXCLAIMED.

I jumped from the bed and turned around to hug the witch. She stiffened under the hug but wrapped her arms around me a moment later. I hadn't realized how much I'd missed the older woman, but the action felt natural.

We separated a moment later, and I returned to my friend's side.

"So... I'm definitely not dead? But Sabine was telling the truth about killing Avery?"

I felt like an idiot for not having thought of it more. My only defense was the gauntlet I'd run through had left me fully depleted.

Hecate nodded once in confirmation.

"Makes me wonder what the difference even is between living and dead then," I mused. "I mean, could we just go back to the realm of the living through another portal?"

Hecate took a step toward me. Her dress today was ornate as usual, but not the most complex gown I'd seen her in. Her hair was wrapped with thin silver chains into a carefully positioned style, her eyes lined in thick black makeup.

"To begin with, what happens when you die. Your friend will be trapped among the stars while you would fall into the pits." A pause, as if she cut herself off from saying more. "And those are the least of the consequences for walking among the mortals."

More talk of consequences without specifics. "I need answers, Hecate." I wasn't sure if it was a demand or a plea. "Cole claims it's too painful to explain, but I'm tired of being kept in the dark."

I expected Hecate to argue, to side with Cole as it seemed she so often did. But instead, she acknowledged my words with another nod. "Very well. But let's not discuss it in this room. I'll find us something more suitable."

She turned back to the exit. Daphne and I exchanged glances, then as one, we started to follow her.

Daphne was dressed in fresh, fitting clothing instead of the dirty rags she'd worn for ages. Hecate looked regal as ever. Whereas I... I was in Cole's shirt.

"Can we grab me some more clothing on the way?"

Hecate turned and cast a critical eye over me.

Then, in a decisive movement, shook her head. "It's not bad for them to see you like this." She turned back and continued to the exit as she explained. "Not all the time, of course, but until a suitable wardrobe is created, this carries a message."

The message was, incorrectly, that I was shacking up with Cole. I wasn't sure how I felt about being the subject of that gossip. Once, I'd been used to constant gossip and mockery in the pack. The months with Cole, with no one else around, had been a unique respite from that brand of torture.

But as we walked through the hallways with Hecate guiding us, no one dared whisper behind their hands this time.

"Why were you locked up anyway?" I asked Daphne as we roamed the halls.

Daphne's expression hardened. "It was right after the Choosing. There was chaos when they ran after you. I wasn't sure what I expected to happen. I tried to run after you, but my father grabbed me and held me back." Resentment sparked in her eyes. "The ceremony continued. No fated mate for me, by the way."

"You're better off without them." I grimaced.

And Daphne, who had once loved Moon-Ghost for all its flaws, nodded in agreement. "I didn't find out more until we got back the next day. Sabine bragged about what she did to you. I attacked her."

I frowned. "That shouldn't have gotten you locked up. Especially as the daughter of the pack Beta."

Daphne almost looked embarrassed. "It wasn't a simple fight for dominance. Avery, I was going to kill her. And... I might have mentioned during the fight I planned to rip Jett's throat out next."

Well. That might've done it.

"You were trapped there ever since the Choosing?" Anger surged inside me. I might have rescued my friend, but there was no justice in it. Not while they lived. Not while they'd locked my friend away for half a year.

Daphne's eyes widened. "Your eyes are doing that thing again." She glanced at my palms and edged away.

I looked down and saw the green sparks playing on my fingertips.

"What 'eye thing'?" Hecate asked, pausing to turn back to us.

Daphne scratched the back of her neck, uncomfortable, and glanced at me for confirmation before speaking.

I nodded. I trusted Hecate, and if something was going on, she might be my only option for figuring it out.

"Her eyes turned green like that when she found me under the Kings's house," Daphne explained.

"My eyes are always green," I protested.

Daphne shook her head. "Not like this. They turned bright green and glowy, and your pupils disappeared."

Hmm was all Hecate said before turning back around and continuing down the hallway.

Guess, in her mind, it was nothing to worry about.

I wasn't sure where we were going, but ultimately, we wound up in a small dining room. By the fact all the food on it remained stationary and we had to pour our wine the old-fashioned way, it apparently wasn't an enchanted table like the one at Hecate's palace.

"Can we get some answers now?" I asked as we sat. The witch was not to be rushed. I may not have known her as long as I had Cole, but I felt that down to the soles of my feet.

"And food," Daphne added with a sheepish glance my way. "But definitely answers first."

I bit down on the anger that rode me all over again at the thought of my best friend on the brink of starvation for months.

Hecate served herself, and we followed suit.

And then, at last, she spoke.

"The male you know as Cole is indeed the King of Hell. That much, you'd figured out."

I nodded.

"You might know it, but you don't truly comprehend its meaning. Hell is more than a simple plane like your realm. Its very existence is magical, drawing strength from all the souls that come to it. And that strength, in turn, is lent to its rulers when they take the mantle."

"So you're saying Cole is strong." That wasn't exactly news.

Hecate arched a brow at the interruption and I bit my lip, promising myself to hold any other statements or questions until the end, lest she decide to stop sharing. "The Cole you knew is but a shadow of the King of Hell. To start, you met him in that isolated plane. It was part of Hell, yes, like your fingernail is part of your fist. By exiling himself to live there, he cut himself off from his true strength. In returning to his seat of power, he's restored much of what he had."

Much, but not all, she seemed to say. I thought back to Cole *poofing* Daphne away. Hecate had said Cole was hopeless in the arcane arts, but that had seemed pretty magical. A sign of just how much power he had here?

And then there was the way he'd rescued us. I'd suspected we had some link, so it made sense he could somehow, magically find me, I guess.

"But he opened a portal. I thought only demons could open portals."

I slammed my mouth shut as I realized I hadn't managed to keep my resolve for even a few minutes. But I had so, so many questions when it came to that male.

But Hecate didn't chastise me, not even with a flicker of her expression. Instead, she nodded in acknowledgment. "Libra demons. And Cole, in his seat of power. But that was not without consequences, Soteria."

"Why do you call her that?" Daphne asked.

I'd just accepted people struggled to say my name. In Moon-Ghost, I was the Omega bitch. To Cole, little wolf. Another person, another name.

"It's a title," Hecate said, turning her head towards my friend, though her body remained facing me.

"Is it because of what Cole said about me having been his queen?"

Daphne jerked back and spun towards me wide-eyed. I shrugged in apology.

Hecate dipped her head in acknowledgment. "It does. But I do not think you are yet ready to hear why."

I frowned, but before I could argue, Hecate continued.

"As I was saying, though he has power here, there is a cost. When you took the moonstone, it was not without consequences. In order to return to his seat, the entire pocket realm was destroyed."

I just stared. Surely I had misheard her.

At my expression, Hecate gave an unbothered shrug and took another sip from her wine chalice. "Think of it this way. The moonstone was a key to a locked door, and it remained locked after you left. Cole couldn't get to the capital with the door shut. So he ripped it apart at its foundation, and with it, the rest of the pocket realm."

A sense of grief slammed into me. That castle had been the only home I'd ever truly known. The house I'd lived in as a Moon-Ghost reject hadn't held a candle to it. The ever-full kitchen. The gym I'd spent hours training in.

The library. I mourned the library, the books, the most.

And then a wave of horror hit me at my shortsightedness.

"There were people there." Maybe it wasn't exactly right, but the murder mermaids, the demons that lived in the fore st... they'd existed.

Hecate waved my concern away with a dismissive hand. "It's hardly a loss. And he would do far, far more to get you back this time."

The implications rocked me. This time.

He killed all of them. Yes, most of the creatures there had tried to kill me if we discounted the rabbits I'd caught in the woods.

But to die? Like that?

And yet, as I looked at my best friend, who was currently doing her best to stay caught up with our conversation, I knew with a pitiless certainty I would do it all again to rescue her. I couldn't exactly claim the high ground here.

And he had rescued me. I would've died all over again, this time with Daphne, if he had stayed in his pocket realm and left us there.

"If this is his 'seat of power' or whatever, why did he even leave the capital to begin with?"

Hecate's tone didn't change when she said a moment later, "Heavy is the head and heart that wears the crown."

Great. That explained *everything*.

"None of this makes sense," I complained. "I appreciate this, but I'm even more confused than I was before. How did Cole become the King of Hell? Why am I even in Hell to begin with if when Daphne dies she's supposed to go among the stars? How is she here now?"

"I second about half of those," Daphne chimed in.

"She is here because you walked through a portal. That is not simple magic. The demons do so through a blood covenant. Your destiny will always lead you to Hell. And as for how he became King—"

"That's enough."

The words were quiet thunder.

Just like that, Cole appeared in the room as if made from smoke. He solidified, his eyes blazing in accusation.

The male who had doted on me for days while only being a little infuriating was gone.

In his place, the King of Hell stood.

I sprung up from my seat. "You can't just forbid her from explaining things when you won't answer my questions."

"Actually," Cole said in a tone that told me I was going to want to strangle him. "I can. That's what it means to be king and for her to be my adviser."

"I was simply going to say that's something to ask him," Hecate said primly.

We both ignored her. I took a step toward Cole. "Oh? Because you've answered so many of my questions before?"

"I gave you all the information you required at the time."

"You didn't give me *any* information," I accused.

"Maybe if you hadn't run off like an angry child, I could have."

"Angry child?" I snarled. "I needed to rescue my best

friend."

"Then you should've come to *me*," Cole growled.

"So after all this time, you would've helped me make a portal to get back to the realm of the living?"

"Not a chance," Cole scoffed. "But I could've found a way. *If* you had trusted me. Instead, we're stuck with the consequences."

"Which are?" I demanded.

No answer. I looked at Hecate. "Well? I'm *sick* of hearing about these unmentionable consequences. I got my best friend back. I can't be sorry for that. I *can't*."

I couldn't. Because if I didn't trust myself in this, I would need to think about what had led me here.

I'd killed a man in the process. A crappy one. Maddox wasn't exactly a benevolent ruler where I was concerned. But he had cared about the pack and almost everyone in it. He'd been the Alpha for as long as I'd been alive, longer even, but he had so much more life to live.

Suddenly, it hit me. I'd shoved it aside while I'd been focused on surviving, on seeing Daphne after recovering. I'd been in a bubble.

And that bubble had suddenly popped.

Arms wrapped around me, a comforting scent I could barely taste as I hyperventilated. Darkness against my face I could bury myself in.

Daphne? A calloused finger wiped the tears I'd barely registered away. *Cole.*

"Shhh," he said.

The world was quiet, just me and my breaths.

"Come with me," he whispered in my ear.

And we disappeared.

CHAPTER XV

I TREMBLED IN COLE'S embrace.

It was a whole-body sensation. My arms were weak as I clutched him. My throat wobbled, words suddenly beyond my grasp. My legs shook, even though I became aware I was seated on Cole's lap.

He had me completely ensconced against him. My entire world was his scent, his body heat. It flooded into me, a comforting thing, but not enough to douse the nausea that grew in my belly.

I wanted it to be enough. To breathe for a moment and remember myself and shove this humiliating episode aside.

My body rebelled.

I pushed off Cole's lap, unstable as I wobbled across the room. We were back in Cole's bedroom, his teleportation having happened in the span of a blink.

The bathroom was clear and lit. I wasted no time or dignity, throwing my head immediately into the toilet.

I wished I could blame it on the transport, but Cole's poofing hadn't given me any of the dizziness the portal hopping did. No, this was something deeper. Something that had been brewing and unearthed itself at an inopportune moment.

Cole was behind me. When the bile finally passed, I'd feel shame at having acted like this in front of him, but for the moment, all I could focus on was expelling every rotten bit of food in my stomach. Cole held my unbound hair back, protecting the strands from my vomit. He placed another hand on the small of my back, rubbing in small circles.

Eventually, I had nothing left to throw up. I hadn't eaten much, but still, my body felt dirty.

"You're okay." The word was not a gentle platitude, but a command. Even now, Cole would order me around.

My lips twitched into a smile, despite my remaining unease.

He helped me up and produced a clean cloth, wiping my face away. I turned away from the intimacy to the sink to rinse my mouth, but my body was still weak. I clutched the rim of the counter for support.

Cole was behind me in an instant. His hands gripped my hips, not clawing, but firm enough to steady me while I washed away the taste of bile. I met his eyes in the mirror. I expected judgment or pity. I didn't know which would be worse.

But there was none. Only a steady existence.

"I was fine a day ago." I didn't mean for the words to come out so quietly, but my voice felt raw after what had just happened.

"You weren't." A gentle blow. "You were surviving minute by minute. Your mind needed space to process and accept the events of the past few days."

"I killed someone."

My voice cracked on the last word. The steadying breath I attempted to draw into my lungs failed to deliver any relief. Cole said nothing to rush me. "I was willing to kill to protect her. I went there knowing that. I thought I could handle it. And he wasn't a good person. I know that. He was a terrible Alpha. Maybe not to everyone, but to me. And Daphne. He just... He had her in a cell. He said he would... he would..."

I couldn't even make myself say the words. My eyes screwed shut, trying to stop the tears.

He turned me around to face him, pressing my back against the edge of the counter while one hand caressed my cheek. I forced my eyes to open again at his silent command.

"Yes, he was despicable. But the Alpha was also a fixture in your life. Someone you'd known since you were a pup. Little wolf, there is no shame in finding unpleasantness in meting out death. I wish I could say it was the only time you will have to face such brutality, but lying to you is the one thing I cannot bear."

He tilted my head up. I didn't fight the action.

"You were fighting for your life. For your friend. And you won. Whatever the consequences, I'm proud of you, Avery."

This time, it was me who kissed Cole.

It wasn't an explosive, passionate kiss. But it was desperate. I'd been drowning, and Cole was the clean air that filled my lungs.

He lifted me onto the countertop edge and my legs wrapped around him, drawing him close. The shirt rode up, and my exposed heat pressed against his crotch, the fabric of his pants an inconvenient barrier.

Moon, I wanted this male. We'd shared a room, sometimes a bed, for days without contact. He had been close, sometimes inches away, but never broke that invisible wall.

But now he did. His fingers dug into my sides in a deliciously possessive way while he tasted me. It was a slow demand that made me yield. I sank into the heady sensation. Instead of devouring me, he seemed to savor my taste, a flick of his tongue making me gasp. It was a comfort I wanted to sink in, a security I'd never had before in my life. I'd been worried he would be furious if he ever saw me again. Now, I tasted how silly I'd been. Because Cole cared. He infuriated me with his sardonic teasing, drove me mad with his refusal to answer questions, but above all, he cared for me in a way no one ever had in my entire life.

It was Cole who pulled away. His thumb rose to my lower lids, brushing the dried tear track.

"Feeling better?"

I nodded. The heightened emotions that had consumed

me minutes before had eased. Now, all I had was a bone-weary exhaustion that belied the fact I'd spent the past four days resting in bed.

As if sensing my thoughts, he adjusted his grip to better support me. "Your body will not recover in an instant. You used a lot of power, both in shifting, fighting, and casting your magic. You'll need to build your stamina."

"How do you know about the magic?" I asked.

Cole shrugged. "We're linked. It's barely a spider's thread, but when you use a big enough pulse, I'm... aware."

Should I be able to feel Cole the same way then?

Cole used my silence as a chance to carry me over to the bed. But from his grip and expression, he wasn't looking to advance what we'd started in the bathroom. No, the male had a single-minded focus to see me rested and whole.

"I can bunk with Daphne," I protested. I was fatigued, but I could sense I wasn't about to pass out for four days again.

The single shake of Cole's head told me what the response to that argument would be.

"Fine," I said before he could open his mouth to say something all possessive like *there's nowhere in this castle you'll sleep except my room*, which would be way entitled and over the line and make my stomach twist in ways entirely different from the way it had in the bathroom. "But I need *actual* clothes then." I gestured to the black silk shirt. Which might have been a mistake because, in our little make-out session, several buttons had opened to the point I was nearly flashing my goods right at Cole.

The wolfish grin he cast over me said he enjoyed the view. But he didn't deny the request. "Anything you want shall be yours."

"Anything but answers," I pointed out.

"In time, you'll know all. Let that be enough." A plea. A demand.

I sighed back onto the pillow, tossing an arm over my head. I was tired of having the same argument over and over again. "As long as I'm ignorant, I can't be with you, Cole." Maybe it was presumptuous of me. Maybe he'd laugh and say this was all physical, deny what I felt between us.

But he didn't. I glanced up, shifting my arm higher.

He nodded.

Then he settled on the bed next to me. Not touching. Not pulling me in. The bed was large enough for both of us, yet my inner wolf howled at the distance.

"Do you trust me, Avery?"

Trust was complicated. Did I trust Cole with my life? Yes.

But could I *fully* trust him if I didn't know him, secrets and all? No.

"Somewhat," I hedged.

He didn't protest. "Trust this, little wolf. You will be safe here, and whatever shreds of your trust or affection you choose to share with me, I'll take until earn them all."

But as I'd soon learn, not everyone was happy to have me here.

CHAPTER XVI

T HE NEXT DAY, I convinced Cole to let me out to explore the city.

It wasn't without an argument. First, that I shouldn't go at all, then that he should come with me, then that if he couldn't come, Hecate should.

But in the end, I won. I argued I wasn't going to be cooped up in a castle (again), that he definitely had kingly duties to attend to, and that I didn't need a babysitter.

"Besides, I'll have Daphne with me, a proper shifter without any defects," I joked to ease the tension riding his shoulders.

It had the opposite effect. "You have no *defects*," he hissed, "save a little too much stubbornness."

I beamed at him. "Then if I have no defects, I'll have no trouble protecting myself and can go out and explore the city."

He acquiesced. The open air of the capital tasted like victory.

The truth was, I had a goal. I was going to get answers

about this place one way or another. I hadn't found Hecate since that first day, and though Cole answered some questions about the land itself, he was cagey when it came to how I fit in. Sometimes, when I pushed too far, he got an inconsolable look in his eyes that made my heart ache. It wasn't him being manipulative, that I was certain of. But something had clearly hurt his past so deeply that even remembering it was painful.

I loathed seeing him in pain.

I'd gathered that the realm I'd stumbled into upon dying had been nothing more than a slight pocket realm, as Hecate had said. It was unclear how I'd even landed there, but I suspected it had to do with my connection to Cole. I'd thought that space was huge, but Hell itself was unbelievably vast. The true realm was so vast it bordered on endless. The capital was the main city, but there were others, though none especially large. While there was a degree of trade and commerce, Hell was not suited for stability. He alluded to the fact that, once, that had been different. Now, the city only managed a measure of peace because Cole was there to enforce it.

My determination to leave also came from a desire to get out of the palace. Oh, it was large and very nice, but I couldn't shake the sense people were watching me. The whispers had dimmed since the first days, and on the occasion I'd stopped to question someone, they refused to say anything that might get them in trouble, from what I gathered. Which, with Cole's volatile temper, could be anything.

Of course, if I'd thought that I would blend in on the streets of the capital, I was sorely mistaken. In the palace itself, people regarded me with hidden curiosity, a mix of mistrust, and natural caution.

There was nothing hidden about the looks Daphne and I received as we crossed the palace threshold and walked among the streets.

"Let's check out the market," I told Daphne, thinking back to the bazaar I'd gone to when I'd first come to the city. Maybe I could find the secret keeper again and bargain with the cat for more answers.

We were both clothed in modern styles. True to my demands, when I'd awoken that morning, the wardrobe had contained clothing my size and taste, just like the magical wardrobe back in the other palace had provided. Simple black leggings, a ribbed tank top, a leather jacket, and solid boots. Daphne wore a similar outfit with jeans, boots, and a long-sleeved tee.

Our clothing didn't exactly have us blending in, but we didn't stand out either. The denizens of Hell were in an unnatural mix of styles. Some wore modern clothing like Daphne and I wore, while others wore distinctly older fashions. Not by a decade, but by centuries. Others, like Cole, tended to wear classic pieces that were harder to place and could be older or newer depending on the cut of the fabric.

"I can't get over this place," Daphne mused, openly taking

in our surroundings. "It's so *big*."

Honestly, she'd taken being in Hell much better than I'd expected. We chatted like it was old times as we walked, like it was the most natural thing in the world for us to be in this magical metropolis instead of the Moon-Ghost territory that had been our entire world.

"It's pretty cool," I agreed.

We reached the edge of the market and began to examine the stalls. Once again, I felt the stares and whispers, but I did my best to tune them out. It was easier with the bustle of the city noises drowning out the bulk of them while vendors called out to sell their wares and haggle with customers.

"They're obsessed with you," Daphne murmured.

I nodded reluctantly. For a lifetime, I'd wanted to be invisible and occasionally succeeded. There was no chance of success here.

Worse, there was also no sign of the cat's tent. Instead, we browsed the aisles.

We paused at one stall to admire the jewelry. Daphne examined a pair of earrings, which were useless since our healing ability wouldn't actually let us pierce our ears, while my attention was drawn to a necklace on the edge of the stand.

"You like?" the shopkeeper asked. He was a gruff-looking male, maybe two feet tall, though he stood on a stool behind the counter, bringing him up to my shoulders. His face was covered in a braided beard that reached halfway down the stool.

I smiled in response, feeling a bit awkward. "It's lovely."

And it was. In fact, it was the most exquisite piece of jewelry I'd ever seen. Gold wire wrapped around small, red stones at varying lengths, dropping down the centerpiece which re-sembled the inside of a geode, with more red stones of rough cut on display.

"Oh, that is nice," Daphne said, looking away from the rings she'd switched her attention to. "It would look great with your hair."

The shopkeeper made noises of agreement, sensing our interest.

"It's magical. The chain is enchanted not to break and would expand to accommodate any shape changing. The ru-bies were harvested from the far lands of this realm and are said to help hone one's natural gifts." He pushed the holder towards me. "Try it on."

"Oh, I shouldn't," I protested, but Daphne simply plucked the necklace from the holder and moved around.

The shopkeeper held up a broken mirror shard for me to examine myself once it was secured.

I had to admit, I liked the necklace. Still, I reached behind so I could unlatch the chain.

"It looks so good on you, miss. You should take it."

"I have no money," I explained.

"No, no," the shopkeeper chastised me with outstretched

hands. "No charge. A gift from a humble citizen of the kingdom to our queen."

I froze. "I'm not the queen."

"Keep it. I will not take it back on my table now that you've worn it," the shopkeeper insisted.

The interaction left me more unsettled than all the whispering in and out of the palace.

Daphne didn't seem half as troubled as we walked about. We looked at several other stalls, but I didn't allow us to linger. The last thing I wanted was more gifts.

Then again, half the stalls had things I didn't even want to touch. Potions, poisons, animal carcasses. Wares were as easily macabre as they were beautiful.

"How've you been feeling with everything?" I asked Daphne softly as we went about.

My best friend shrugged. "It's a lot, but it could be worse, right? I haven't sensed any danger since being here. I mean, I'm being treated better here than I was by my own pack."

The bitterness in Daphne's words was a blade to my own heart. "What happened with your parents?"

"Disowned me." She tried to dismiss it with another shrug, but the hurt in her words was palpable. "Not at first, but when I wouldn't back down and apologize, they said I wasn't fit to be their packmate, let alone their daughter."

She paused at a stall to gather her thoughts under the guise of examining some fabrics.

"I think it was simple self-preservation more than genuine loathing. My dad's always been quick to heel when Maddox said the word, and my mom fell in line with him. I've known I've been without a pack for half a year, so it's not totally fresh. It's just different now to wonder what I'll do if I'm no longer resigned to dying in that shitty cell."

I squeezed her hand in comfort. Daphne was never half the pessimist I was, and the loss of her family, and pack, grieved her.

"I don't regret any of it though," she said, pulsing my hand back. "You're my pack, Avery."

"Mine too, and... I mean, as long as Cole doesn't get sick of me and kick me out, you'll always have a place here. And even if he does, we'll find our own palace to take over. Since they seem to grow on trees here."

Daphne grinned. "Oh, I don't think there's any danger of him kicking you out. If anything, it seems like he wants to lock you away in his rooms and never let you out."

I flushed. "He's just protective and got used to taking care of me."

"Sure," Daphne said in a voice that told me she believed that lie about as much as I did. "He keeps you wearing his clothes and flips out at the mention of anyone going near you because he's a *naturally protective Alpha*. That's why everyone was terrified to go near his room while you were recovering. You know the kitchen maids were drawing straws for who would have to drop off supplies and get yelled at if the soup was a hair too hot or they lingered a second too long?"

"How do you know that?"

She tapped her ear. "Shifter hearing, remember? Besides, the nurses in the sick ward liked to gossip. I wasn't so bad off, so I mostly laid there and listened, especially since they kept insisting I wouldn't be allowed to see you no matter how much I pestered them."

I hadn't known any of that. Had Cole—cool, collected Cole—really been that temperamental about my care? Or maybe he was just naturally scary and they were exaggerating.

"Speaking of, when did you get so strong? You used to be weak as an infant, no offense, but you were holding your own against Maddox like a sentinel."

"None taken. I don't know, when I died... it was like something clicked. I can shift easily. I can fight. I mean, Cole trained me, like I told you. But I'm just naturally stronger now too, like a regular shifter."

"You can shift here?" she said with interest.

I nodded. "It's... incredible. It's like having a part of my soul back."

"Oh." Daphne was silent for a second. "That's interesting. Because I can't feel my wolf at all."

CHAPTER XVII

"**W**HAT!"

"Shh," Daphne said, casting her eyes about with suspicion at the attention my outburst had drawn.

It made sense. A shifter who couldn't access their wolf was as good as defenseless, as I well knew from personal experience. And even though I felt safe here, it was almost certainly a false sense of security.

She tugged me farther along until the crowd lost interest in us.

"What do you mean you can't feel your wolf?"

"I just... I don't feel anything. I can't shift. I have my normal shifter senses, but I can't call on my wolf side. Can't change shape, not even my teeth. I assumed it was the same for you."

I shook my head. "No. If anything, I feel more in tune with my wolf here than anywhere else." Even now, my wolf was hungry to come out and play.

Daphne shrugged it off, but it obviously bothered her. "Maybe it's because I'm not really dead. I don't know. There's a magical explanation for everything here, and too much we don't know."

On that, I agreed.

Daphne didn't want to discuss it any further, so I dropped it and we continued around. When we hit a food cart, both our stomachs growled as we eyed the gyrating spits of meat.

"You two ladies hungry?" the meat seller asked.

"Absolutely," Daphne said, not making any attempt to hide her interest.

"Just three gold pieces each," the shopkeeper replied.

There was a gleam in his eyes and a twist of his lips that made me suspect he was playing a trick, like the price was much lower and he was exploiting tourists. Of course, I had no clue what a gold piece was worth or how much the meat should cost.

Not that it mattered. He could charge us one piece together or ten each and my answer would be the same. "We'll pass. We don't have any—"

"Put it on the King's tab," my best friend cut me off, giving him a winning grin.

"Daphne," I hissed as the meat seller turned to shave off some meat for us. "You can't just put things on Cole's tab."

"Why not? If he knew you were hungry, don't you think he'd want you to eat?"

Okay, yes, Cole definitely had a thing about making sure I ate, but that wasn't the point. "Still. We could just go back to the palace for lunch."

"Do you *want* to go back?" Daphne countered.

No. I was enjoying the freedom, being out and about instead of seconds from being whisked away and locked in Cole's room again. I wanted to keep exploring the city. It made it so obvious that Moon-Ghost had been a paltry town in comparison. I'd never considered myself to have any amount of wanderlust beyond an ache to escape my abusive pack, but the city was electrifying. Dangerous, yet enthralling.

"I don't want people to think I'm his sugar baby or something," I grumbled while we took the meat. It was wrapped in a flatbread and I bit into it because, despite all my protests, it smelled delicious and I was famished.

"How about his queen?"

I nearly choked on the bite I'd taken. Daphne gave me a laughing glance before taking a bite of her own.

We left the bazaar and wandered around the rest of the city. I knew from my travels that outside the city gates, there were other settlements. I desperately wanted to learn more about the city, yet I had so many questions I barely knew what to ask. Sometimes we just wandered about, listening to town gossip. The sky was the burnt red of evening when we wandered into a tavern.

Thankfully, this one wasn't blocked by a giant.

"Can I remind you we don't have any money for drinks?" I didn't want to put anything else on Cole's tab.

She waved aside my concern. "Hecate gave me some money before we left." She flashed a handful of coins in her pocket.

I looked at her, aghast. "Daphne! If you had money, why didn't you pay for the food?"

Also, why hadn't Hecate given me money? Not that I was entitled to it, but still.

She grinned. "Hecate gave the money as a backup, but it was her idea to put things on your sugar boo's tab. I just wanted to see your face when I did that."

"Brat." I rolled my eyes.

"You love me," she said with a laugh as we strolled into the bar.

Immediately, the atmosphere shifted. Outside, we'd been regarded with cautious suspicion. Here, the air had turned hostile.

My instincts, as ever with danger, were to flee.

But I was tired of running. It was probably nothing anyway, and if it wasn't, Daphne and I could handle it.

Maybe. Daphne couldn't shift. And both Cole and Hecate kept reminding me if anything happened to me, I'd face eternal torment after dying again.

But running felt *wrong*. So when Daphne gave me a questioning look, I strode over to the bar and pulled out a stool to sit. Daphne slid into the seat next to me.

The bartender regarded us from across the divide with something bordering on contempt. She was a portly woman who would've looked normal if not for the ox horns protruding from her plaited hair.

I flashed her a winning smile. Fuck being scared or snubbed.

"Wha'dya want?" the barkeep said, walking over with loud steps against the wood floor.

"Two beers." I suspected they didn't have the fruity cocktails Daphne and I had previously dabbled in.

Daphne slid a couple of coins across the countertop.

The bartender looked at them with open distaste.

"Is there a problem?" Daphne asked.

"No problem," the barkeep spat before swiping the coins off the counter. "Always happy to serve the whims of the crown. When you're here, why not get drunk?"

I refused to flinch at the acidity in her tone. Who had pissed in her cereal?

She turned away. Daphne and I exchanged another look. *What is her problem?* she mouthed.

I shrugged.

Our drinks were planted in front of us with a slam a moment later.

I sniffed mine. It was probably fine, but I wouldn't put it past the woman to have spit in it.

Or worse.

"What, too good to drink my ale?" the barkeep snapped.

"Too good to even show up the past century," a customer

growled.

"Look at them, acting like they can walk wherever they please," another slurred.

"Stupid to wander in here. King doesn't know everything that goes on." A third voice.

Chairs moved. The tension shifted, growing into a solid weight.

Daphne twisted around to cover my back while I refused to take my eyes off the bartender.

"Friendly place you got here."

"Not for you," she huffed.

Then she walked away. For the briefest second, I thought it might be to defuse the tension.

But once she disappeared behind a curtain, that just signaled to everyone else that it was open season on us. More patrons stood. Not everyone, but enough to form a small crowd around us. The leers turned to steps.

"Gonna teach them a lesson," the original voice hissed.

I stood. Daphne did the same, pressing her back to me.

Then, someone made a move. It was a tall, brutish-looking male with at least two feet on me and a hundred pounds of muscle. He started toward me, a glass lifted in his hand either as a haphazard weapon or simply because he was too focused to put it down. He lurched forward. I braced, ready to defend myself.

But he never reached me. Instead, one second he was moving for me. The next, his body split in two, falling to the ground while blood splattered everywhere.

"Come now, gentlemen. Is that any way to treat your future queen?"

The voice was familiar. I stared at the creature that stood behind the would-be attacker. A black-skinned male with constellations etched on his skin stood, wiping the blood off his blade with the shirt of the recently slain body.

Phaidros.

CHAPTER XVIII

"P HAIDROS."

The Libra demon winked at me over the mutilated corpse of the ogre. "Hello again, love."

It was a warmer reception than I'd gotten from the demon last time. A couple of weeks ago, I'd had to make a nuisance of myself and plead with the male to make a portal to get back to the realm of the living.

I turned myself toward Phaidros. The demon wore simple leather garments over a puffed white shirt that opened into a deep vee that revealed the stars tattooed on his skin, a more casual appearance than what he'd sported the last time I saw him. He still had too-pretty features, yet they clashed with the three-foot-long blade he was cleaning with the ogre's shirt. His own clothes were miraculously spotless, without a speck of blood on him.

Though I focused on Phaidros, who was clearly the biggest threat here, I kept an eye on the rest of the would-be attackers. Yet at Phaidros's quick dispatch of the ogre, the rest dispersed, gone back to their tables and mugs of ale as quickly as they'd risen. The air was wet with hostility and blood, but no one dared look at me.

The tension didn't ease out of my muscles despite the threat passing. Especially not when Phaidros stepped over the corpse and settled into the seat next to me.

"Betsy! Another ale, please," the demon called out as if he hadn't just vanquished a foe three times his size in the span of a breath.

The barkeep, who had fled to let Daphne and me fend for ourselves, reappeared with an uneasy grin and placed a cup in front of Phaidros without a word before settling on the other end of the bar.

My lip curled in contempt.

"Who is this?" Daphne murmured in my ear.

"Name's Phaidros, love," the Libra demon said, fixing his attention on Daphne.

And it was quite a bit of attention. His eyes roamed her body, taking in each curve with an appreciative gleam in his eye.

My mouth contorted into a silent snarl again.

"A thousand pardons. Didn't realize you were so jealous of my attentions." Another wink. A careless swig of alcohol. Phaidros set the mug down with a satisfied exhale.

I wasn't jealous of the demon's blatant lust for my best friend. But I didn't trust him. If he turned that sword on me, I'd have no defense against it. My fur was sturdy, but it wouldn't survive solid steel.

"Join an old friend, won't you?"

With nothing better to do, I sat in my original seat. Daphne followed my lead.

"I'd hardly call us friends. But I guess it's all relative." I cast another glance back to the room, but no one seemed the slightest bit interested in us now that Phaidros had clearly positioned himself as an ally.

Was he someone powerful? When I'd found him before, he was sitting in the dark corner of a tavern by himself. He hadn't seemed especially serious, just a bit dismissive with his devil-may-care attitude.

"Truer words!" Phaidros lifted his cup to toast the two of us. I lifted my own mug but didn't take a sip before setting it down.

He glanced at my mug with a frown, snatched it, and took a sip before spitting the liquid out a fraction of a second later.

"Hey!"

"Don't drink that," he commanded.

I bit back a growl at being ordered. I'd had enough of males ordering me about for a lifetime. "Wasn't planning on it."

"Betsy!" Phaidros called again. "Two cups of ale. Without the jonquil powder, if you wouldn't mind."

The barkeep's eyes widened in shock before nodding.

"Jonquil?" Daphne asked.

I frowned. "It's a poisonous plant. Not lethal though."

Phaidros gave me a look as if I'd done something he hadn't expected before quickly recovering. "Quite right. No one here would *actually* try to kill you, even that heaping pile of flesh."

He jerked his thumb back to the still oozing body behind him. My gaze slid over it and back to the demon.

"Didn't seem that way when he was charging for us," Daphne huffed.

Phaidros waved away her concern with a careless gesture. "Rest assured, they're stupid lifeforms, but no one is *that* stupid and survives."

I gave a pointed glance over his shoulder.

He shrugged, as if admitting the point. "Okay, he might have started to get carried away. Probably self-preservation would've won out, but in any case, I figured I'd do a good turn and eliminate the issue."

"How charitable," I murmured.

Truth was, the entire thing was fast and violent, and I'd barely processed it. One moment, there was a threat and the next, it was gone. I should've been grateful, but all I had was the uneasy sense a greater threat had taken its place.

"Not a charitable bone in my body," the demon chirped.

Now *that* I believed.

Betsy returned a second later with two fresh mugs in front of Daphne and me. She swiped the others away and refused to make eye contact.

"Sorry about the mistake. Was a complete accident," she

said before shuffling away.

Yes, the poisoned plant had slipped into the mugs all on its own. I didn't understand the reason for her animosity, but when I sniffed the ale, it smelled normal. I decided to risk a sip.

"What do you mean by *that* stupid?" Daphne asked pointedly.

He lifted his mug to gesture to me. "To try and kill her. Anyone with a shred of intelligence in this realm sees red hair and pays proper respect. Or gets butchered. Either is acceptable to the king, I suppose."

My red hair. I'd been the only wolf I'd ever seen with it across the packs. In Moon-Ghost, it had been a feature others scorned. Unnatural. Made some speculate about my parentage, especially since my mother never mentioned my father. It drew attention when I'd rather sink into the background, and worst of all, it marked me as an outsider.

Yet I'd had reactions even in Hell to my hair. In fact, when I'd seen Phaidros, it was only once my hood fell—revealing that hair—that he'd bothered to give me the time of day. I cast a wary glance toward him. At the time, I had been so focused on Daphne that I hadn't bothered to consider what had changed his mind. Yet now, I wondered. Clearly, my hair signified something.

A feature I'd shared with Cole's previous queen? That would explain why it inspired both scorn and gifts, like in the case that Daphne and I went through the bazaar. I fingered the pendant resting between my collarbones absently.

"It certainly doesn't make me popular."

"There are reasons for that," Phaidros answered, ever cryptic.

"I wish I knew those reasons." Frustration colored my words.

"I could tell you," Phaidros offered. "Not for free," he continued when my gaze turned suspicious. "But I'd wager I can fill in a lot of the gaps that are likely bothering you, better than just about anyone but the king."

"How would you know so much?"

His answering grin was all teeth. Handsome, no doubt, but it reminded me of the fangs of a viper when it stretched its mouth wide before striking. "You could say I know a bit more than the average demon."

"Okay. Tell me why everyone hates me." This would be a great conversation for my self-esteem.

"Not for free," Phaidros repeated. "And I'll remind you, you already owe me one favor."

Right. The favor I'd agreed to for a portal. Of course, I hadn't planned to come back to Hell, so I hadn't expected the demon to ever collect.

"I have gold coins to pay with."

Daphne slid a few over the counter in my direction, but Phaidros didn't spare them so much as a glance.

"Don't insult me, love. I'm hardly going to give these answers up for simple money." His face broke into a grin as he continued, "My price is another favor to be named by me at a later date."

"A *small* favor," I countered. "Nothing violent or dangerous, not to me or anyone else."

Phaidros hemmed and hawed for several moments as if considering, but I'd seen his eyes when I bartered. He knew he had me hooked and was just reeling me in.

Still, I wanted answers. So I could only hope I wouldn't regret this when he finally settled and offered me his palm. "Deal."

We shook.

"Good. Now tell me why everyone hates me."

CHAPTER XIX

T HE DEMON ARCHED A brow at me as he took another leisurely sip of his ale before setting it down and turning fully toward me.

"How much do you know?"

It was a gamble. Was he pumping me for information?

In any case, my gut was not to fully trust Phaidros. He'd helped me, but as he said, he wasn't prone to any altruistic tendencies. "Assume I know nothing." It was probably close enough to the truth.

"Very well." Phaidros cast a glance to the neighboring tables and flicked his wrist, the stars etched on his skin dancing in the motion.

The noise around us dampened. "What did you do?" Nothing looked different, but my skin tingled.

"Just because you're paying for information doesn't mean everyone else gets to hear it for free. Besides, I'd assumed you'd want some privacy for this, and short of trekking a few miles outside the city, a noise-canceling spell is about the best protection you can get from curious ears."

Magic, as I'd suspected. The book I'd read on demons had only mentioned portals as being part of the Libra demon domain. "Can all demons do this?"

A flash of pearly white teeth. "As I said, I'm not just any demon."

I wasn't about to trade more favors for clarification, so I urged him back to the task at hand.

"So why do they hate me?"

"They resent you for leaving them behind."

"But I never left them," I grumbled. What did that even mean?

"I suppose when I say 'you' it's a bit murky. You share the same soul as the old queen, after all."

This was what Cole had hinted at a few times. "So they think I'm her?"

"You're the same soul," Phaidros repeated. "But even the same soul born twice into the same circumstances will be different, and obviously, yours is quite different. I couldn't speak to your previous personality, but I'd expect you to share several core traits and values, but not identical. Your previous incarnation was considered rather charming from what I recall, and you don't quite pull that off."

I'd bargained a favor for a personality critique on how I wasn't Miss Manners. Somebody kill me again.

"Physically, though, you're identical." The demon looked my features over from head to toe. Not leering, but it made me want to recoil all the same. "I'm sure that's quite confusing for your former husband."

I jerked back. "Cole was my husband?"

Phaidros nodded. "He didn't go by that name then. The king left this plane and went who knows where, visiting only intermittently through the following decades."

Either Phaidros was playing dumb, or he really didn't know where Cole had gone. Still, I was reeling from the revelation. He'd called me his queen, but no one had been willing to elaborate on what that had meant.

"And that was when I left?" I asked, trying to piece together what I'd learned in the past with these new revelations.

Another nod, as if he wasn't leveling my understanding at this very moment. "I can't speak to the precise reasons for your demise, but I gather there was a terrible amount of self-sacrifice involved when you cast yourself to Tartarus. Of course, that bit of information is tip-top secret." A cheerful wink. "So, with the general public not knowing the reason their queen disappeared after ruling for a millennium and you showing up all willy-nilly like a teenager, some are a bit touchy. Others are simply trying to ingratiate themselves with you." He tipped his cup towards my necklace, which even now I fingered while I tried to take in everything he'd just told me.

There was no point in correcting the fact I wasn't a teenager but rather twenty-one, if I counted my time in Hell, when he'd just told me I'd ruled with Cole for a thousand years. And gone to the pits.

"How do I know any of this is true?" I demanded. "I don't remember any of this."

That earned an eye roll. "The whole point of reincarnation is to forget everything. You're your own person, but you're shackled to your past, which, unfortunately for you, is quite substantial. It's not all bad. You were known for being a beautiful, fair queen and tempering the Lord of the Underworld's more ruthless tendencies. The black of death balanced by the red of lifeblood, as it were."

He continued before I could interrupt and ask what he meant by that. "If you have any doubts about what I said, ask your king. He can confirm everything I said with ease. Though he may not be pleased that you heard it from *me*." He gave a shrug, as if he didn't care what Cole thought of him.

I wasn't sure that was wise, given that I'd seen Cole rip apart creatures with ease that the three-foot sword at Phaidros's hip would envy.

He flicked his wrist back up without another word, the quiet rumble of the tavern returning to its previous din.

"Question time is over. I'll be collecting this favor within a week, love. And I expect *prompt* payment."

Phaidros was gone.

And I wondered if I'd come to regret this exchange not just for the price I'd pay but for what I'd received.

I T WAS LATE IN the evening by the time Daphne and I made our way back to the castle.

Daphne disappeared shortly after we crossed the threshold. I didn't blame her for needing time to herself. I appraised the glances of the staff as I made my way to the bedroom. Phaidros's words had answered a lot of questions I'd had. Several things clicked into place. The deference I was regarded with in the castle halls, the mix of suspicion that went beyond just being under Cole's protection. The reluctance they all showed when it came to approaching me. Did it make sense I was being held accountable for actions I couldn't recall, a life I didn't remember? No. But my years of torment in Moon-Ghost had taught me to keep my expectations of others low.

Cole was coming down the hall from the other way, dressed for a day in court, doing whatever Kings of Hell did. I offered a tentative wave in greeting.

His nostrils flared.

Suddenly, Cole wasn't at the other end of the hall. He was right in front of me, imperious gaze bearing down on me.

"Why," he said with deceptive calm, "do you smell like blood?"

Oh. I inhaled, realizing the slaughter at the bar had left a stain. The same breath drew his scent in closer to me, drawing my wolf to the surface. She really liked how Cole smelled.

Annoyed at my wolf, I rolled my eyes. "Because I haven't showered yet."

That was the exact wrong thing to say. Cole moved forward, and suddenly I was pressed against a wall.

"Who?"

The entire hall seemed to shake from the word.

"It wasn't a name-exchanging situation." I lifted my chin, refusing to be intimidated by his theatrics.

The hallway shook again. The chandeliers shaking as Cole loosened a growl.

Okay. Maybe it was a little more than theatrics.

"You'll take me to them, and I'll rip their heads from their bodies. And then I'll post their bodies on the castle as a warning." His voice turned more animalistic at the end of the threat, his own wolf clearly riding him.

Well, that was graphic. I mean, it wasn't my version of hospitality, but that was Cole. Mr. Manners.

"They're already dead," I assured him. "I dealt with it."

I opted to leave out the part about the demon being the actual one to kill them. Somehow, I didn't think that would help calm Cole down.

The hallway stopped shaking. Or rather, the little earthquake moved from the hallway to my stomach as Cole lifted a hand to my cheek as if he had to see for himself if I was alright.

"I'm okay," I said softly.

He didn't drop his hand, simply shifted it down to my neck, a gentle press on the side where he could feel my pulse.

"I will kill anyone who attempts to harm you."

Words I had longed for my entire life, but if I'd learned anything, it was that there was no guarantee anyone could protect you. "I can take care of myself."

Cole obviously didn't like that answer, but I didn't have the energy to argue.

"Look. All I want to do is take a shower and pass out."

Cole was silent for a moment. Then, in an elegant move, he stepped back and gestured to the door of our room a dozen paces away. "As you wish."

My eyes widened in surprise that Cole would drop the issue and let me have the last word on it.

I should have known better.

No sooner did I close my eyes to sleep than I found myself in another shared dream.

I'd woken by lakes of lava, unending fields, mountains, even the castle. This time, our setting was a simple field.

And Cole was directly in front of me. Shirtless.

I stumbled back, and he caught me with ease, even though it wasn't possible to actually hurt myself in a dream.

"Careful, little wolf."

"Why aren't you wearing a shirt?" I tilted my head up to force my attention to stay on his face rather than the expanse of

muscles that was in front of me.

"I could ask you the same question, but I'm not complaining."
I jerked my head down.

"Perv!" I snapped. I was in nothing more than a bra and panties, both made of lace that left little to the imagination.

Had Cole seen me naked? Yes. But somehow, the lingerie left me feeling even more exposed.

"All the better for me to inspect you for injuries. After your excursion today." His eyes flashed.

"That doesn't even make sense," I hissed. I crossed my arms over my chest, fighting the flush that was quickly rising on my cheeks.

He cocked a brow in challenge. "It's your dream, little wolf. If you don't like how you're dressed, change it."

"This"— I dropped one arm to gesture down—"was not my idea."

"Maybe not consciously."

"You're infuriating."

"If you mind so much, change it. It's your dream, after all." He smirked. "Or if you just want to even things out, I can take these off." He gestured to his trousers.

"That. Will not. Be necessary." If I really was in control of this dream... I imagined myself in normal clothes. Nothing. I tried reaching with my magic, though...

For a moment, nothing happened. Then, a moment later, I had my workout gear on.

Much better.

He shrugged like it was nothing to him, and glanced around the field. "No bed this time?"

"The bed wasn't my doing either! And I didn't know these dreams were real. And you didn't tell me." It wasn't just the humiliation that angered me, it was the fact that Cole always knew so much more than I did and refused to share that knowledge. "You don't tell me anything. You didn't tell me I'm supposedly a reincarnation of the old queen of Hell that everyone hates!"

Cole stiffened. "Who told you that?"

I growled. "So it's true? The question isn't who told me, it's why didn't you tell me? You said I was once your queen, but at every chance since, you've refused to give me any more answers!"

"Who, Avery?"

Now who had questions? "You have a lot of nerve demanding answers when you still refuse to give me any."

"Because I'm protecting you, you frustrating female," Cole growled. "Haven't you heard ignorance is bliss?"

"I've heard knowledge is power," I snarled. "And I've been powerless for far too long. You don't tell me shit, and then I have ogres wanting to beat me up and bartenders poisoning my drinks! This doesn't keep me safe, you stubborn jerk. It makes me vulnerable!"

The transformation over the setting was instant. Cole may claim I was in charge of the dreams, but there was no denying the very sky darkened at the mention of danger.

"You'll tell me where this happened, and I will deal with it."

"I dealt with it."

"Did you?" Cole challenged. "Because I received no word of a massacre, and that's exactly what such behavior warrants."

"You want me to kill everyone who gives me a dirty look?" I snapped.

"No." For a second, his gaze softened. "I want you to tell me when it happens so I can do that."

The words were crazy. Yet they were also affectionate, which was the weirdest thing.

I didn't want affection. I wasn't done arguing. "How many times do I have to tell you? I can protect myself."

"Can you?" Cole scoffed, obviously indicating the contrary, and if I was in my wolf form, my hackles would have risen. "You need training."

"You trained me for months. Are you saying you weren't up to snuff?"

"I trained you in the basics of being a shifter. Not combat," Cole countered. "And those who would do you harm have centuries of training for you to compete with."

"Who, Cole? Who wants to harm me, and why?"

Cole ignored the question. "You need training."

"Fine, set me up with a guard or something, but tell me why." I hated that I felt like I was begging for scraps.

His eyes flashed. "No other male will train you."

"Well, I'm not training with you. Not while you keep being so damn cryptic about everything."

Cole stepped forward, closing the small amount of space I'd carved between us. "If you refuse to train, you will only move with a full guard."

"I don't need babysitters!" Okay, maybe Daphne and I would've been in big trouble if Phaidros hadn't shown up, but the last thing I wanted was more people who thought I was the old evil queen or something watching my every move. And I did want to train. But right now, allowing Cole to do so, sinking back into old patterns, would be giving in. Like before, when I'd let him keep me ignorant. He'd had more secrets than I'd ever imagined, starting with being the king of the entire freaking r ealm.

"Then I simply won't allow you to leave the palace."

"Allow?" I growled. "No one allows me to do anything, Cole. I'll come and go as I damn well please."

Cole leaned in. "If you think I won't chain you to our room to keep you from falling into more trouble, you're sorely mistaken, little wolf. Train or find out."

"I'll train with Hecate."

"She can't teach you everything you need to know," he snapped.

"No, but at least she tells me some things. Tell me, Cole, since I've come back, what is one piece of information you've given me?" Fury coated my words. "Tell me about my past life. Our *past. Why the people hate me. Anything, dammit. Just stop keeping me in the dark!"*

Something like guilt crossed his face, but it was gone too quickly, replaced with resolve. "I'll tell you this, Avery. Everything I do, everything I have ever done, has been to keep you safe. And if I've learned anything in my long life, you make that task exceptionally difficult."

Infuriating male!

"If that's the best you can do," I snarled, "then I want you out of my dreams."

And then I managed something I'd never attempted before.

I shoved Cole out of my dream.

CHAPTER XX

After our dream argument, Cole spoke to me in the morning to say I could continue to train with Hecate—for now—and then disappeared.

And that was just about the last I saw of him.

I told myself it was good. He was keeping secrets, and I was still mad at him. You'd think that meant I was seeing him regularly since we shared a bed, but it didn't feel that way. Some nights he wasn't there by the time I fell asleep, nor when I woke up to resume my lessons with Hecate. But the pillow would be fresh with his scent as if he'd slept there and I'd never noticed.

If I didn't know better, I'd say he was avoiding me.

My training with Hecate ramped up. She didn't just restart our lessons from before but mixed in an education on a wide range of topics from magic to court politics. We started early in the day and worked until the afternoon when Hecate had to tend to other responsibilities. There were still topics she declined to answer about, no doubt due to Cole forbidding it, but at least I felt like I was developing an understanding of the realm around me.

Despite Phaidros's ominous parting words, the next few days fell into an uneventful routine. Before our fight, I'd resolved to ask Cole about sword training, but now it felt like submitting to his demand to train me without any concessions on his part. And my pride wouldn't allow that.

The magical lessons with Hecate were easier than they'd ever been before. I wasn't going to be any kind of enchantress anytime soon, but I could more reliably call the green sparks forward. At first, they were just light. Under Hecate's guidance, they crackled with electricity. Weapons.

To my surprise, scrying was now off-limits. Once, on a whim, I'd mentioned wanting to look back at the Moon-Ghost pack to see what had become of my old pack under Jett's rule. Call it *morbid* curiosity—acquired after dying.

"Absolutely not," Hecate said, harsher than I'd ever heard her.

"Why?" Before, she'd encouraged me to try any and every type of magic. "Isn't it harmless?"

The witch shook her head. "Scrying is a window. And the wrong forces may look back. It's best to keep you hidden here."

"Who am I hiding from?" Jett certainly didn't seem powerful enough to come to Hell to exact any revenge. He almost certainly didn't even know the realm existed since it wasn't part of shifter lore, or at least not the kind I'd ever been taught.

"It's better for you not to know."

I'd have screamed, but Hecate seemed almost apologetic at the admission.

Secrets. Always so many secrets.

I made the mistake of mentioning healing myself to Hecate, but I wasn't able to replicate it.

The witch was kind, but I suspected if not for the threat of Cole, she would've slashed me wide open to see if that would spur me on.

We set healing aside, but she turned to more advanced lessons. In a matter of days, I could turn pebbles into roses and grow bushes from dirt. Not exactly useful magic, but it was a victory when, before, everything had seemed utterly out of my grasp.

The lessons beyond magic were also interesting. She educated me on the order of the palace, introducing me to different members of the court who treated both of us—Hecate, really—with the utmost deference. And it was those visits that showed me Cole's true place at the top of the palace. The people spoke of him with reverence in their voices. The reverence did nothing to mask the unmistakable odor of fear.

Cole really was the King of Hell.

The fact I wasn't walking around in a shirt of his hadn't diminished the looks and whispers in the slightest. Then again, now I knew there were even more reasons for them.

"It's like they expect me to do a party trick," I grumbled after we walked away from another stilted introduction. This had been with Cole's captain of the guard, Stefan. The man looked to be a few decades older than me, the age wearing on him as if he knew his time was coming and would face it with dignity. Yet, unless someone killed him, he'd live forever in this realm.

He'd declined to shake my hand, just regarded me with a slight bow before updating Hecate on something I didn't understand and turning away with another backward glance towards me.

"No doubt they do," Hecate said with a wry smile, leading me back to the large training space she'd commandeered for the past couple of days. Whatever it had been before, it now was only ever occupied by the two of us. It was a square courtyard, about fifty feet on each edge, with three floors above winding around it. People occasionally paused on the railings above to watch, but I followed Hecate's example and ignored them.

She gestured towards a dead tree, a fixture in the courtyard we'd danced around while I'd focused on smaller tasks. To-day's challenge—make it bloom. I turned my attention to it, trying to recall her many lessons. To not force the tree to act against its nature, but make it want to bloom. It was harder than usual since the tree was utterly dead. I could turn stones into flowers through transformation, but this was a different magic. Rebirth. Something she'd tested me on before and I'd failed miserably.

"It's good your powers are growing, Soteria," Hecate said as I pressed my palms against the tree, trying to find an entry point. "You'll need it for when you become his queen again."

CHAPTER XXI

I swung around at her words, breaking contact with the tree and shattering the little bit of progress I'd managed.

"Um, run that by me again. Was that a joke?"

"Did it sound like a joke?" Hecate asked in a confused tone.

I wasn't fooled. Hecate had a habit of revealing bits of information in a careless way, like telling me Cole was the King of Hell, all the while being completely aware of what she was doing.

"You're saying I have to *marry* Cole?"

The enchantress shrugged. "It's a boon if the ruling couple is joined in such a way, but it's hardly required. The crown follows power, not matrimony."

"Then wouldn't that make *you* queen?"

Hecate laughed at that. "It doesn't work that way. My power is not the kind meant for ruling." She turned to face the tree. "Alas, I could spend a hundred days trying to give new life to this tree, but it would reject every attempt. Soteria, this is *your* domain. Even the king himself would fail here."

"What if I can't? I know you all seem to think I'm the reincarnation of Cole's old queen, but I'm just *me*. A shifter reject." The old wound surfaced, an ache of longing, of not being good enough. I didn't know if it was worse for no one to ever expect anything of me except to serve as a punching bag or to face impossible expectations. They'd thickened in the air, the people always watching and observing. On the occasion Daphne and I had gone back into town, it was impossible to miss. As much as I loved the city, I'd begun to feel like a failure just by walking around.

"Do not doubt yourself in this, Soteria." She slid her hand over mine, drawing it to the tree. "You have more power than you know if you'd only claim it. It is crucial you do. This tree is like the realm. Dead. Decaying. But it was not always like this, and you can stop it from descending into rot for eternity. The path of souls has been disrupted, the cycles malformed." At my look of confusion, she shook her head. "It will make sense in time. For now, spend your days here. Practice your magic. Learn the people and they will grow to love you as this tree will grow anew once you harness your magic."

Her hand slid off mine. I pressed my hand into the withered bark, trying to draw at tendrils of magic as if I could force new life into the tree. Frustration gnawed at me. Failure. The taste of it was bitter on my tongue.

Bitter and familiar.

"You will learn, Soteria. But I fear you must do it quickly."

I flicked my eyes to her. "Why?"

It was rare for Hecate to avoid my gaze. Now, the witch focused her attention on the tree, as if it held all the answers. "Consequences, Avery. *Everything* has consequences. That which came to pass a hundred years ago haunts us. As does what occurred a month ago. I can only hope we will all be prepared."

With that, Hecate left me in a puff of purple smoke. Another ominous end to a conversation. I should make business cards that said AVERY WARD: RECIPIENT OF VAGUE BAD NEWS AND REINCARNATION OF THE FORMER QUEEN OF HELL.

I refocused my attention on the tree. Although Hecate seldom gave me complete answers, she was probably my most reliable source of information. And if she said I needed to learn to master this skill, well, I wasn't doing anything else particularly useful with my time in Hell. I spent the rest of the morning and most of the afternoon focused on the tree.

There was something to the tree, something I couldn't grasp. Daphne found me hours later, sweat pouring down my back as I pressed my palms against the nearly petrified bark over and over, trying to create new life where there was none.

But failure remained my constant companion. It dogged me all day, and when I fell asleep, once more alone in that massive bed, I wondered if Cole was as disappointed in me as I was in myself.

But when I awoke, he wasn't there for me to ask either.

Instead, there was a letter slipped under the edge of the door with my name on it.

CHAPTER XXII

I ROSE FROM THE bed in a hurry once I spied the letter by the door. Could it be from Cole?

It had been days since I'd seen Cole. Apparently, my urging him to return to his unspecified kingly duties had been taken a bit too seriously.

I kind of missed the grump.

Scratch that. I missed him like I'd miss a limb, constantly reaching for it and somehow handicapped by the phantom loss. Even though everything told me it was unwise to want more from Cole, that there were too many secrets, too many unnamed threats for me to explore whatever attraction there was between us, it was no good. My chest ached anyway.

I picked up the letter and flipped it open so quickly I cut my hand on the stiff paper. The wound sealed in seconds, but blood decorated the edges of the parchment. I didn't care.

Disappointment sliced through me as I read it.

It was immediately obvious the letter was not from Cole.

In his own way, Cole was giving me space, but in the brief months of training, he'd become a fixture in my life.

I read the note in more detail, committing the words to memory.

Hello love,

Time to pay up on that little favor you owe me. As agreed, I won't require you to hurt yourself or anyone else. All I ask is for a little bit of gardening. You must first make a purchase on my behalf. Go to the stall marked by midnight blue fabric and tell the female named Hia you've come to pick something up for me. You will, of course, need to provide payment. This is between you and Hia, but you'll find her fair enough to deal with. Once you have the package, plant it in the ground a half mile past the gates.

You have until midnight.

The note was unsigned, but the sender was obvious.

Phaidros.

I frowned at the note. What purpose could this little bit of gardening do? There was obviously more to it, but I had to honor my word. And hope Phaidros was telling the truth.

I debated asking Hecate about the note during training, but I worried she'd rat me out to Cole, who would freak at the thought of me leaving the capital, even for a little bit.

Instead, I sought Daphne the moment our training ended. She was spending time in court and had taken up a habit of flirting with whoever she came across in the hallways. For me, it had the added benefit of adding a layer to my education of court politics as Daphne relayed bits of information they shared with her. People were more open with her than me, with my red hair serving as a scarlet letter. For Daphne, the bit of flirting sometimes turned into entertaining ways to spend her nights.

I grabbed her away from her latest conquest and practically shoved the note in front of her.

I didn't have to say anything. One shared glance with Daphne and we were on our way out of the palace.

Navigating the city was easier each time we did it. I loved the bustle of the city, though I could have easily lived without the stares we continued to receive. The bazaar was all the way across from the palace, by the gates, so it took easily half an hour to get there. And that was only the beginning of the trip.

I'd been back to the marketplace a few times, but it was no easier to navigate this time compared to the first. The tents seemed to shift with every visit. Phaidros hadn't exactly tripped over himself to provide concrete directions, but that was fine. It gave Daphne and me time to wander around. I had until midnight to meet his deadline, but I wanted to tackle it as soon as possible. The sooner I could wipe the slate clean between us, the better.

Being in debt to a demon just didn't seem smart. A necessary evil, perhaps, but not smart.

"Stop! Thief!" someone called.

Daphne and I spun in unison at the shouting.

"Thief!" A larger figure ran after the supposed thief.

"Someone stop him!"

A short figure barreled forward, weaving around a crowd of indifferent onlookers.

The figure was getting closer and closer. At the last minute, I moved, sticking my foot out to trip the would-be thief and catching him by a skinny arm.

I blinked.

"It's a kid," Daphne said, echoing my thoughts.

Children weren't a common sight in Hell. I spent the half-second before the shopkeeper caught up pondering exactly how this child had wound up as a thief in the underworld.

"Thanks"—*pant*—"for"—*pant*—"catching him." The words stumbled from the merchant as he reached us. A baker, by the look of his flour-stained apron. He was a portly figure with a big beer gut and short stature that made him look rather round, in sharp contrast to the kid whose arm I gripped that was barely skin and bones.

Said kid was currently trying, and failing, to yank himself out of my grip.

I knew the moment the merchant recognized me. His gaze flicked to my hair and then back to me.

I recognized it now after talking to Phaidros. The looks were uncertain and uncomfortable. Once, in their minds, I had been their queen. Now, I was an unknown. "Um, sorry to trouble you. I'll take the delinquent off your hands."

He made a move to grab the child, who flinched. On instinct, I pushed myself between the baker and the child.

"Just a minute. Do you mind telling me what happened?"

I looked to the boy for an answer, but he kept silent, biting his lip. He couldn't have been more than ten.

"No need to trouble yourself with that, m'lady. I'll see that he's dealt with appropriately." An angry glint in the baker's eye told me that there would likely be a beating involved.

"I insist." I let a trace of Cole's all-commanding voice slip into my voice, lending the demand of authority I lacked. "What did he steal?"

People paused to watch the spectacle, but I kept my gaze fixed firmly on the baker until he looked away, submitting. "Show her, boy. Don't shame yourself further."

The boy didn't look at me. He just raised a shaky arm in front of me and unclenched his fist.

Bread. All he'd taken was a bit of bread.

"Is this all?" Anger seeped into my words. "It's barely a mouthful of bread. You chased him for *this*?"

The baker took a step back. "It's the principle, you understand. You let them get away with these bits of mischief and they'll get up to all sorts of issues. Gotta discipline them."

The only reason I didn't growl was that I thought it might scare the child.

Instead, I turned my attention to the kid, kneeling down in front, relaxing my grip on his arm. "What's your name?" I asked, keeping my voice soft.

The boy worried his lip with a tooth before answering. The baker looked about ready to bark an order at him, but I shut him up with a glare. "Dario."

"Dario. That's a nice name."

The boy gave me a tentative smile, but it fell off his face the moment he glanced back toward the baker.

"I'm Avery," I said, refocusing his attention on me. "Can you give this man back the bread you stole?"

Dario cast a mournful glance at the mouthful of bread he'd swiped. His stomach growled, and my heart broke. How was it there were rooms of enchanted food in this realm but the boy was starving? But Dario did as I asked, and the baker swiped the scrap of bread up immediately.

"You can go now." My voice was cold as winter nights when I addressed the baker.

He hesitated only another moment before trudging off.

"I'm sorry I stole," Dario spoke with a slight lisp.

"Nothing to be sorry for." I couldn't bring myself to chide someone for taking care of themselves.

It reminded me of all the times I'd come back to my house in Moon-Ghost. The fridge was empty, more often than not. My mother never bothered to pick up our allotted rations, not concerning herself with needing to provide for me. The scant container of orange juice that taunted me more than once came to mind.

It wasn't right. It wasn't right what had happened to me, and it wasn't right what had happened to Dario.

An idea took shape. I could taste the citrus on my tongue.

Dario's eyes went wide. I released his arm, closing my eyes to focus, but he didn't run.

"Avery, is that you doing that?" Daphne gasped.

I opened my eyes a moment later.

There, in the middle of the marketplace, was a fruit tree. It was taller than a normal tree, towering over us by at least thirty feet. People had to move back to give it space. I'd have felt bad if not for the fact that the market seemed to constantly rearrange itself. It could handle doing so around a random tree. The ring of onlookers stared at the tree.

Hecate would be proud, I mused. I hadn't meant to make an entire tree. I'd just thought about an orange. My magic had acted on its own, finding life deep in the ground and spurring it into a tree. Even now, with my magic, I could feel the roots, the branches, the leaves. The tree was solid, as if it had sprouted in this spot decades ago and had seen several seasons instead of just the bleak red sky of Hell.

I reached up and plucked the freshest orange from a low-hanging branch, and handed it to Dario. His eyes widened at the sight of the fruit, looking back and forth from me to the fruit.

I nodded in permission.

And then he took a giant bite of the orange.

"No, no." I laughed and showed him how to peel the fruit. "Here."

He devoured the orange, then looked up at the tree in a silent request. I plucked a few more, ignoring the growing whispers around.

Dario ate two more whole oranges before his stomach was satisfied and then requested more for his pockets.

"You can have as many as you want," I assured him, plucking another orange to split with Daphne. "And then we can head back to the palace. I'll make sure they set you up with *proper* food."

Dario stared at me for a moment when I said the word palace.

And then he *poofed* out of existence.

CHAPTER XXIII

AT MY OBVIOUS PANIC over the disappearing child, one of the onlookers explained that the "child" was an imp. Forever young, forever hungry. They had been unconcerned and then quickly scattered upon my distress.

There might have been some growling involved on my side.

There was nothing more to be done, so Daphne and I continued on our quest to find the stall. Blue tents were in surprisingly short supply. Up and down the aisles we went, scanning, searching.

It was halfway through the afternoon when we found a tent matching Phaidros's description. Midnight blue fabric swooped low, covering all but the narrowest opening. I pushed the material back with my hand and walked in.

The fabric shut behind me with a snap. I spun at the sound. No Daphne.

Did Phaidros lead me to a trap? I pulled and pushed, but it didn't budge.

"One customer at a time, dear."

I turned back and was face-to-face with a woman who was

far, far too close.

Her hair was spun silver, the strands braided back with several wiry strands falling out to frame her face. Her skin was wrinkled as if she was days away from death, yet her eyes were lively, sparkling in the limited light of the tent.

"You're Hia." It came out as an accusation.

"Indeed." She stepped back and extended a bangled hand in my direction. "And you're the former queen."

"Debatable. Let my companion in."

She cackled. "Hardly a debate when you're giving orders like you're in any position to make demands." She moved around the space, unconcerned.

It was unlike any of the other stalls I'd seen. Some were open, some covered in fabric, but most had a similar structure. A long table and chair for the merchant to use. Hia's tent was chaos. Wooden shelves that looked far too permanent for a tent surrounded all walls, save the small gap of the fabric I'd come in, as well as a door in the back that couldn't possibly go anywhere without the use of magic. The shelves were lined with everything from worn books to trinkets I couldn't name.

"In the marketplace, all are equals, kings and peasants alike, if they wish to make bargains. And in my domain, I deal with one bargainer at a time." She cast a knowing look toward me while caressing a shelf. "You seek one, do you not?"

"I do." I disliked being separated from Daphne, but so far, it seemed Hia was more eccentric than murderous.

Then again, it was Hell. Lowering your guard for even a moment was always a mistake. "I'm here on behalf of Phaidros to pick up some seeds."

If Hia was surprised by the request, she didn't show it. "Naturally. I have what you—or I should say, the demon—desire. It's a matter of payment on your side."

"I don't suppose you take gold coins?"

At the wry shake of her head, I sighed. It was never so easy.

"What do you want then?"

Hia looked at me, appraising. "What to ask of our former queen?"

"I make a mean pumpkin bread." It wasn't exactly a lie, if by "mean" you meant "gag-inducing."

Another cackle. "I'll decline that this time. No, my price for what you seek is this. You must be bound to one form for three days. You will not be able to shift, no matter what you attempt."

I kept my features neutral. Could it really be that easy? I hadn't shifted forms yet since being back. What were another three days?

"Deal," I said quickly before Hia could change her mind. "Where are the seeds?"

She gave a careless swipe from a shelf and produced a pouch. She held it over my outstretched hand and then snapped it back when I reached for it.

"The price will come once they are planted. Understood?"

I nodded, and she finally handed the pouch over. Unable to resist a peek, I undid the drawstring and spilled the contents into my palm.

"Teeth? I came for seeds."

"You came for what Phaidros wanted you to plant," Hia corrected.

The teeth were large, about three inches wide at the top and five inches long. Whatever they had belonged to had been big.

"Plant them no less than a foot deep and four feet apart," Hia instructed.

"Full sun or partial?"

"There is no sun in Hell."

My career as a comedian was over before it had a chance to begin.

I left the tent without the mystical fabric obstructing me and found Daphne waiting outside, not looking half as worried as I expected. I held up the pouch in triumph, though a thread of unease worked through my stomach.

"Wow, that was fast. What, did they just hand you the seeds when you walked in?"

I frowned. "I was in there for a while."

Daphne shook her head. "It was barely five seconds, Avery."

Clearly, whatever happened in that tent took place on a different time scale. It didn't perturb me half as much as it should have. I was growing increasingly used to the unusual magics of the realm.

"Let's get this over with."

We followed Phaidros's instructions and made our way out of the city.

It was my first time outside the walls since I'd first come to the city. We walked until I was confident we'd hit almost a mile from the gates. The area was more sparsely populated compared to the city, but there were small settlements stretching out.

"Too bad we don't have a shovel." Daphne began to roll up her sleeves, but I shook my head.

I flashed a grin at her. "Watch this."

I placed my hands down on the ground, feeling the texture slide against my palms. I shut my eyes. Took a breath.

And then I summoned my magic.

It wasn't an uncontrolled burst, not like what I'd produced before. Here, my magic was a scalpel. The dirt was hard-packed, but when I opened my eyes, there were three perfect holes, matching Hia's specifications exactly.

"Well, that was handy."

It was no teleportation, but I'd take what I could get. I pulled the pouch out of my pocket and extracted the three teeth for the holes. Once again, I drew on my magic and recovered the holes.

Before I fully closed them, I hesitated. There was something there. Something that reminded me of the petrified tree Hecate had sent me against. Dead, yes... but still there. Deep.

My magic wanted to do more, but I couldn't figure out what *more* was.

The second I lifted my hands from the ground, my body twitched.

No.

And it hit me; I knew I'd agreed to Hia's deal too quickly, because while we agreed I would spend the next three days bound to one form, we had never agreed on which one.

And apparently, I was spending the next seventy-two hours as a wolf.

CHAPTER XXIV

*H*OME.

The thought slammed into my wolf mind. It was more than a word. It was a prayer. It was salvation. The air tasted right in Hell, in a way the realm of the living hadn't. The last time I'd shifted, I'd been fighting. I'd been angry.

Now, instead, there was just intense longing. Desire.

Need.

And my human mind, in horror, knew exactly what that would mean.

I couldn't force my wolf to even slow enough to try and communicate with Daphne. The second my four paws hit the freshly planted ground, I spun back toward the city walls and took off in a run.

Because my wolf had one priority above all others.

I was a blur of crimson. As a human, my red hair drew uncertain looks in the capital. As a wolf, I distantly registered the stunned looks as I passed through the crowds. The people of Hell jumped out of my way as I passed, something my wolf distantly recognized with a shred of pride. She enjoyed the recognition.

But that was nothing, barely a wisp, compared to the pulsing demand to get to *him*.

I was fully aware of what was happening, but I had no control over my wolf. No influence. Whatever shred of harmony I'd struck upon in combat flew away when I tried to say, *Hey, wolf-self, maybe play it cool and hide out until the next three days pass.*

You'd think getting back into the palace as a wolf, sans opposable thumbs or the ability to speak, would be hard, but people took one look at the four-foot-tall red wolf and got out of the way. No one stopped me as I ran through the palace halls in search of him.

Then again, it was for the best. If anyone tried to stop her from getting to Cole...

It would be bloody.

I found him by scent, an instinct so deeply buried, so long slumbering, I'd never known it was there.

I hadn't shifted once since coming back to Hell, and I knew I was about to get a harsh reminder of why.

And then my search ended.

I walked into what could only be a throne room. The walls were lined with soldiers, the room filled with courtiers and other well-dressed people. At the back of the room, in the center of a large low dais, were two twin thrones of onyx. One sat empty.

And on the other was the King of Hell, as I'd never seen him before.

There he was.

Cole.

It had been days since I'd laid eyes on him.

And he was magnificent.

He wore clothes more elegant than I was used to seeing him in. An ornate coat covered the usual simple silk shirts he favored. Every inch of his clothing said wealth. His hair was pulled back, a crown resting on it. He filled the room with his presence. He was justice and danger, a barely contained storm sitting on a throne.

There could be no doubt, not in this moment, that he was the ruler of the realm.

He sat, one ankle crossed over his knee while his head rested on his fist as he leaned back at whatever he was listening to. A bored expression lined his face.

Until it fell to me.

Surprise was masked as quickly as it flashed, the slight narrowing of amber eyes, the barest tightening of his jaw.

My wolf had hesitated for the barest second before surging forward to take her rightful place at his side.

Please don't ask for a belly rub, please don't ask for a belly rub, I pleaded with my wolf-side.

Hecate was at his side, a step behind the throne. My wolf loosed a low growl at the woman—not genuine anger, but a warning. With a wry look in her eyes, she moved farther away.

The wolf, mercy of all, didn't roll over on the spot. Instead, she—*I*—settled into a seated position next to Cole and dropped my head to Cole's knee. Possessive. Marking the male as mine.

I couldn't see Cole's expression from this angle—instead, my wolf stared down every attendant of this impromptu reunion.

And then, *bliss*.

Cole's hand caressed my ear, the perfect pressure as he scratched the sensitive skin there.

No.

No, don't do it.

But he kept caressing.

He did it, like everything else, so perfectly. Like he knew exactly how to extract just the right feelings from me.

I heard it more than felt it.

Powerless to stop it.

Thump, thump, thump.

My leg involuntarily gave in to the instinctive relief.

I'd murder him when I turned back into a human. If I didn't die of shame first. He knew *exactly* what he was doing. My wolf continued to look out, making eye contact with each and every one. No one dared laugh.

And then Cole continued to hold court as if nothing was happening.

CHAPTER XXV

T HE HOURS PASSED AS Cole held court. His stroking seldom abated, but I slowly wrangled enough self-control to stop the humiliating thumping and observe.

I settled my attention on the court proceedings. It was fascinating to listen as Cole ordered the court about. He was fair when he heard petitions, not lenient, but fair. I'd had no idea what to expect, but it was clear that Cole didn't simply rule through raw might. Oh, no doubt he was the most powerful creature in the room. But he listened to those who approached him.

It was a completely different side from what I'd ever seen before. I'd seen the flirtatious Cole, the grumpy Cole, even the angry Cole.

But this... this was something else entirely.

At some point, Daphne arrived, clearly having come looking for me. She didn't approach until the court dispersed. My wolf gave her hand a gentle lick, an apology for leaving her behind.

"What happened?" Cole demanded.

I hadn't felt the need to explain the bargain on our way to plant the teeth. Now, I regretted my silence. "I'm not exactly sure."

"She made a deal," Hecate said. She rounded the throne, moving to stand by Daphne as she bent down to me. "Correct, Soteria?"

I dipped my head in confirmation.

"It will fade in a few days, I assume. Nothing to be concerned about, though I'd caution you to be more careful in your dealings."

Cole made a sound of frustration. He twisted to face me, and I lifted my head to meet his gaze from where I still sat.

"When you shift back, I'm going to make you train the likes of which will make the Leo demon look like child's pay."

But it would be a few days before I shifted back.

My wolf refused to be parted from Cole. I joined him at dinner and in bed. There was no sneaking out before I woke the next two days. Instead, I joined him in court again and observed.

The evening of the third, Cole deviated from his normal routine. He changed from his regal work clothes and put on the normal outfit I was accustomed to seeing him in when we went training. Simple, lightweight black clothing.

I twisted my head from where I watched him perched on the bed in question.

Cole read my expressions perfectly, even as a wolf. He

smirked. "We might as well have some fun."

And then Cole teleported us away.

I'd come to learn portals were used for travel between realms, whereas powerful creatures could simply teleport themselves within the realm. That was how Cole kept *poofing* people away at his convenience.

I blinked as I stood on unsteady legs.

The place... it was familiar. The sky was red—still in Hell, after all—but I had been here once before. With a navy sky.

The first time I'd ever seen Cole. Back when I'd thought they were just dreams. I wasn't sure how I could recognize it after all those years when I hadn't even recognized Cole. But this place...

This place was *home*.

I had no words to ask Cole. Surely he knew my questions?

"This is where we first met. Then... and a thousand years before."

I jerked my head back. The human in me wanted to prod and process. He was finally offering information, real information. But my wolf... all she wanted was to see her male.

A mass of sleek black fur came into view. The scent of his fur was thick in the air. My wolf wanted to roll in the scent until it was enmeshed in our own.

Cole may have dressed as a king as a human, but as a wolf, he was a raw, powerful Alpha. Amber eyes met mine. Unflinching.

I met his gaze. There might be a hundred questions between us, but this? This moment felt right.

And then a blur of black bolted ahead.

He ran through the field and I took off after him immediately. It wasn't the sprint of danger, but rather an invitation. The dirt slid between my claws as I bounded after him. My body relished in the release. Weeks of being cooped up in the palace were fine for pampering, but they did nothing to soothe the beast that lived inside my skin.

Did Cole feel the same need I did? He was always so in control, but it was impossible to hold every emotion tightly in your chest when your wolf took over, no matter how harmonized the two souls were.

I caught up with Cole a few beats later. We ran together. Our flanks brushed side by side as we crossed under the dark sky. I had no idea where we were headed, but I was grateful. Cole led us forward through a forest. For hours, we ran and hunted. We shared a pair of rabbits we caught. Cole nudged the scant meal my way first, an act that pleased my wolf to no small degree.

All the while, he watched me.

I never wanted the night to end. I'd never known such simple contentment.

Could this be my life? I wasn't sure if it was the simple nature of my wolf's thinking that led to the thought or simply my own weariness, but in that moment, I felt I would be utterly content if this was to be every night for the rest of my life.

The fact it couldn't be was a simple reality I forced myself to ignore for the rest of the night. I ignored it while we ran, while we nuzzled, while Cole magicked us back to the palace into the bedroom.

I slid into bed, curled up tightly with my tail wrapped around my nose. Cole was next to me. He never said a word, not the entire evening back. Instead, my body pressed against him, savoring the contact. I was doused in Cole's scent, and my wolf never wanted it to fade.

I didn't want it to go either.

I fell asleep with the taste of him over me. The deepest, most peaceful sleep I'd ever had.

When I woke up, I was refreshed. I wanted to stretch my arms and run a dozen miles to start the day.

Except Cole had my body pinned in his embrace.

My human body.

My very naked, very human body pressed against every ridge of him.

CHAPTER XXVI

"**Y**ou're finally awake."

My breath caught in my throat. "You're here."

"Where else would I be?"

Wherever is it you go when I wake up alone. I'd mourned the loss of it for so many days, but did this—the day I'd turned back into my human form after being stuck as a wolf—*have* to be the day Cole picked to stick around?

"Can't you at least pretend to be asleep so I can sneak out of this bed?"

Cole's grip tightened against my torso.

Our bodies were pressed together. And both of us were naked. My face grew hot as I realized exactly what part of Cole was pressed against my back. By the feeling, it was... large. And he was hard.

"So eager to leave me?" His words were a warm caress against my ear.

Every fiber of my being wanted me to curl back into his embrace. To turn over, to roll my hips on top of his and lean over his naked, delicious-smelling body. My nipples hardened into stiff peaks, wanting to be played with.

Shit. *Shit*, I could not do this with Cole right now. Especially not after I just spent the past three days trailing him like a lovesick puppy.

A girl had to have some pride. And falling over myself to be in the arms of a male who had avoided waking up with me despite forcing me to share his room was not going to help with that.

The worst part of it was if he was even half the shifter I knew the King of Hell to be, he wouldn't be able to miss the scent of exactly how much I didn't want to leave this bed.

"I've got, um, things to do today." I tried to wriggle out of his grip, but the slight catch of Cole's breath told me that was going to have the opposite effect desired.

At this, Cole finally released his grip.

"Yes, you do."

He moved out of bed and I was treated to a view of a very sculpted backside along with his winding tattoo as he pulled a discarded pair of slacks on. He turned back on me and I quickly jerked the thin cover over myself.

"You're going to tell me how you got stuck in your wolf form for the past three days." It was the return of his Alpha do-what-I-say-or-else tone.

"I made a deal," I hedged.

The look he gave me had no doubt intimidated many of his subjects. "Tell me what you agreed to."

I sat up because I couldn't stand to have him towering over me while I lay in bed, careful to keep the blanket clutched to my chest.

"You want secrets? I'll show you *mine* if you show me *yours*."

I'd meant to be glib, but when Cole's eyes darkened and dipped to my body, which was barely hidden by the thin blanket, it was immediately obvious where Cole's mind had gone.

And as my gaze roved over every inch of him, my mind went to the same filthy place.

"I should punish you for that insolence."

My mind went further to the gutter.

"By making you run laps," he mused, clearly enjoying the way I got flustered at his innuendo.

"No, no, you're far too busy with your kingly duties for me."

"Oh no, little wolf. For you, I'll *always* make time." The majority of the bed was between us, but it felt like no barrier at all. "It's time to resume your training."

"With Hecate."

"With *me*. If you don't know by now not to make bargains with anyone who offers, then I've given you far too lax a tutor."

The chastisement smarted. *Lax* was the last word I'd use to describe Hecate's teaching style.

Still, I could use some... physical exertion. Running last night in my wolf form reminded me of how much I missed it. The work with Hecate was challenging, but it didn't leave me with the utter exhaustion that a good training session did.

And I had missed this. *So why fight it?*

"Fine. I'll meet you in half an hour." After three days of not showering as a wolf, I was in desperate need of hot water running over my body. "Now, shoo." I waved my hand at Cole.

His lip quirked up. "Only you would shoo away the King of Hell."

"Only because he's a perv who would watch if I didn't."

Cole didn't argue the accusation. He just gave me one final heated look, grabbed a shirt from seemingly nowhere, and left the room.

I wound up taking a cold shower.

Cole was waiting for me down the hall. He was talking to some member of the court who was draped in expensive fabrics and holding a stack of papers, pointing animatedly.

Even in simple slacks and a silk shirt, he looked like a king. In contrast, I'd opted for sweats and a tank top. Cole spotted me instantly but didn't move away.

"What do you think?" he asked me as I approached.

"About what?"

"It's the settlements," the other man explained. He had hair pulled back in a thin ponytail, which did him no favors, considering the wiry gray hairs didn't start until halfway back on his head. In fact, everything about him was gray. His hair, his eyes, even his skin had a vaguely colorless appearance. "They've been complaining about... *disturbances* in the area and want the protection of the walls, but we don't have the resources to expand them, and if we do, it'll take too many resources to manage."

I frowned. "I'm guessing the inns within the city walls don't have enough space for them?" I'd seen only a few small inns while walking through the town.

A nod of confirmation.

"Then tell them if anything happens, they can come to the palace. I'm sure there's more than enough space." It might be cramped, but from what I'd seen, there couldn't be even a thousand people living in the scattered farms around the walls. We could accommodate that.

I expected the courtier to laugh me off for not knowing what I was doing. What did I know about these decisions? But Cole gave me an approving look.

"But... it's not proper," the silver-haired man protested.

I shrugged, my confidence bolstered by Cole's silent agreement. "It wouldn't be *proper* to abandon them. Besides, it would just be temporary, right? And if for any reason they did need more permanent protection, we can look into slowly expanding the walls so that it's not too big a strain."

"That makes sense." The words were almost reluctant.

Gray eyes met Cole's, awaiting confirmation.

"Do as she says," he instructed. "And see to it internal protocols are put in place."

"At once, Your Majesty. I'm grateful for your guidance." The latter half was said to me.

"Wait. What's your name?" I asked. "I'm getting tired of having too many nameless faces floating around."

His eyes widened in surprise before he quickly schooled his features back into neutrality. "Petyr, my lady."

"Petyr. Nice to meet you. I'm Avery." I stretched a hand out.

He bowed, ignoring my hand.

"I will get to work at once."

Cole nodded in approval, dismissing Petyr.

We went down a long hall, a winding staircase, and then reached a part of the palace I'd never seen before. There were guards scattered throughout the palace, wearing uniform fighting leathers. The outstretched dirt ring, with an elevated platform, was obviously where they trained. Entrances lined the ground level, but Cole led us out one level above.

In a fluid movement, he jumped down. I followed, finding him halfway across the training ring before my feet sank into the dry ground.

Without warning, a spark of silver flew my way. My hand stretched out, shifter reflexes and months of training allowing me to catch the foreign object rather than letting it slice me in half.

A sword. Cole had just thrown a three-foot-long, ra-zor-sharp blade at me.

"Let's get started."

Chapter XXVII

THE STEEL BLADE WAS heavy in my hand, the weight unfamiliar when I'd only fought with fists and claws before. Immediately, Phaidros's deadly skill with his wicked sword came to mind.

A new weapon. One I wanted to train with *desperately*. In fact, I'd planned to ask before I'd gotten stuck as a wolf. A coincidence, or could he actually read my mind?

Cole stared me down from across the arena, his own sword held low as he considered the blade.

"Shouldn't we be using practice swords or something?"

"Why bother?" Cole's voice was as nonchalant as ever.

I adjusted my grip on the blade. It was lighter than I'd expected, only a few pounds, but I enjoyed the way it moved in my hands. I held it up to catch the light, examining the edge. The blade was so sharp I imagined in skilled hands it could split a strand of hair in two.

And he'd thrown it at me like it was nothing.

"I could hurt you."

Cole laughed, the sound filling the arena. "You can try,

little wolf."

I glared.

"Besides, we won't be sparring today. As eager as you might be to fight me, you need to first learn the basics."

Okay, that made a *bit* more sense than having the two of us immediately go at it.

"So everyone trains with real steel from the get-go?"

"Not exactly," Cole conceded. "But I think it's prudent to accelerate your training, and you'll learn more by nicking yourself on a real blade, with the real weight behind it, than by using a stick."

There it was again. That undercurrent of urgency that so often came from Cole and Hecate.

I didn't argue the point. Being in that tavern with nothing to defend myself and Daphne with but my own hands and inconsistent magic was frightening.

"Then let's begin."

Cole moved me into position. It started, he explained, with footwork. We spent twenty minutes making sure my feet were positioned just right. From our previous training, I was pretty good at keeping my weight evenly distributed, but the sword work required more precision.

Once that was done, he taught me some basic positions and began to drill me. Block. Dodge. Lunge. Block, dodge, lunge. Over and over until it was nearly a dance. He'd alter the order, critiquing my form if my arm dropped even half an inch too far.

No one fought with weapons in Moon-Ghost. Disputes were settled with fists or fangs, but that made sense when your opponents were also shifters.

I'd never been good at fighting growing up, but the drills came to me quickly. Quicker than even Cole seemed to expect. Sweat dripped on my brow, my muscles aching after hours of repetitive, relentless movement, but the real game was keeping my mind sharp through everything. I found myself enjoying the challenge. It wasn't just that it felt good to move, it was exorcising the restless energy that plagued me. The blade quickly became a natural extension of my hand.

Cole's orders came faster.

"Dodge! Lunge! Parry! Switch! Lunge! Again! High block! Low! Thrust! Dodge!" Cole barked one command after the other, not giving a moment's rest between them. The sequence was new and the longest yet. My muscles screamed, but I ignored the protest and concentrated on meeting his demands.

I executed every movement in time, fighting against an invisible opponent with all my force.

By the time I finished the challenging sequence, I wanted to collapse onto the dirt floor.

To my surprise, a scattered round of applause came from above. For the first time in hours, I looked up at the raised levels.

Cole and I had attracted an audience. Hecate and Daphne had come to watch. But not just them. Others crowded around, peering over the railing to watch. Mainly soldiers, by the look of it. In their gazes was a newfound respect.

"Not bad," Cole said.

High praise from him. I flashed a grin, then lifted my tank top to wipe the sweat from my forehead. My body was slick with it, but I'd never minded. Better sweat than blood.

Cole growled a low sound. I dropped the shirt and looked at him, confused. But his attention wasn't on me, it was on the crowd a row up.

The males up there hastily looked away, busying themselves with whatever was back the way they'd come. Cole's growl faded.

I hid a grin while I swallowed large gulps of water straight from a carafe someone had brought. Was Cole jealous of those other males seeing my exposed stomach? I wasn't sure how it mattered, since only a few days ago, Hecate had advised me that showing off my goods apparently sent a message. Still, the possessive look he flashed my way sent an electric thrill down my spine. It made me want to stand up straight.

"Let's really give them a show." I lifted my blade, flat side up in question to Cole.

"You think you're ready after one day of training?"

"I might not beat you," I agreed, "but I bet I can give you a run for your money. I mean, have you ever had a better student?"

"You're the only one I've ever taught, little wolf."

"So what you're saying is I *am* your best student."

That got a hiss of laughter, finally wiping the dark look off Cole's face from when he kept glancing up at the onlookers.

"You're the best of everything," Cole said.

For one moment, I was weightless.

"But not better than me."

Without warning, he charged. His sword went from a limp blade at his side to a deadly weapon with a flick of his wrist.

Block.

My defense snapped into place. The clang of steel shattered the easy atmosphere. Cole's eyes met mine, the glint of the metal reflecting in his eyes for one precious moment. Then he pushed farther, harder, and I jumped back.

He lunged again. *Dodge.* Lunge. *Dodge.* Lunge. *Block.* I was on the defensive, losing ground with every inch.

This won't do.

I might not be good enough to win, but I'd be damned if I let everyone see Cole back me into a corner without breaking a sweat.

Block. Block. Then, a break in his perfect form. I thrust my blade forward, but he anticipated my movement. His blade met my own, shoving my sword up. The tip of his weapon grazed my tank top as I barely danced away in time.

"Had enough?" he taunted.

"Never." I might be losing, but gods, sparring with Cole was fun. I might never be sure where I stood with him, but here, in this ring? Every moment was electric. The crowd was nothing. It was him, me, and the clash of our weapons, serving as its own secret language.

Our dance resumed. I could counter his strikes, but getting my own in was difficult.

If you can't win, change the game.

He backed me farther and farther. After hours of training, I was exhausted, even with my supernatural stamina. A minute of dueling with Cole was more taxing than an hour of drills. It was no surprise to him that my strength flagged. My shoulders slumped. I kept blocking, but my strikes came slower.

Just fast enough to not be sliced in two.

Cole's lip tipped up. *The bastard liked to win.*

My heel tapped the wall of the stadium. Cornered.

But so do I.

I'd developed quite a taste for it.

So when Cole lifted his blade one final time, intent on pinning me, who was clearly slow and sagging, I did something that shocked him.

With every ounce of energy I had left, I dove the opposite way. His momentum pushed him closer to the wall before he pivoted on his heel to face me, but I was ready. I knocked into his side with the heel of my sword, pushing him off balance and into the wall.

Where I had just sprouted thick green vines from between the cracks in the foundation.

It had been hard to split my attention between acting like I was weakening and summoning my magic. It hadn't been an act at all, really, but a gamble.

But as I watched Cole struggle, his arms pinned high, his legs wrapped in green tendrils, it was all worth it. A vicious grin split over my face.

I win.

"Cheat." There was no malice in the word. Rather, Cole almost sounded impressed.

"Winning is winning," I chirped, my gaze roaming over the male pinned against the wall. For someone so in control, the juxtaposition gave me all kinds of ideas I'd never entertained before.

"Very true." He was no longer struggling in the vines. Instead, he gave the binds a single glance, and to my shock, they began to wither. One second, strong green vines had bound them. By the next breath, they were black and crumbled to the ground.

Where my magic was potent, plentiful life, his was endless death.

The shock bought Cole one second—one crucial second—to advance on me. He kicked off the wall and threw me down, the flat of his blade at my neck.

Chapter XXVIII

One second, I'd been on the cusp of victory.

The next, Cole had once again shown me exactly how big the gap between us was.

I hadn't exactly expected to win, so if I was feeling rational, I'd have been pleased with my performance considering I'd had less than a day of training.

Thinking rationally while Cole had my body pinned under his, the edge of his blade grazing my chin in a way that stopped me from so much as breathing too deep was not something I was capable of.

"Let me up," I demanded.

Cole bent low, never moving his sword so much as a fraction of an inch while his lips grazed the edge of my ear, his messy hair tickling my face.

"But, little wolf, I so enjoy having you pinned under me."

His words hit their mark. My body tensed under him, wanting to push this game of dominance until the end, to argue and then revel in submission when he forced it out of me.

Clearly, my wolf was still far too close to the surface.

"Don't you have someplace better to be?"

"Never," Cole answered immediately.

But he did ease up. "However, if you don't stop wriggling under me, we're going to be very, very late for the ball."

I forced my body to freeze in place. "What ball?"

Cole flashed a grin at me, enjoying my surprise. He withdrew his sword, the weight gone as quickly as it had been pressed against me. He held out a hand to help me up, and I took it, still off-kilter from our match.

"The one that had to be postponed because the guest of honor was stuck as a wolf." A knowing look.

In my honor?

"Anyway, there's late and fashionably late, and no doubt your friend has been waiting impatiently for us to finish so the two of you can get ready together."

Sure enough, when I finally tore my gaze away from Cole and glanced up, Daphne was gesticulating pointedly on the upper level. The entire act included arms thrown up, tapping the invisible watch on her wrist, and a heavy sigh.

Daphne was big on punctuality.

We retreated back to the bedroom I shared with Cole to get ready. It was disconcerting to see another person in the space, even if it was my best friend. In all the time I'd spent at the palace, I'd never seen or scented another person inside it. The room was always tidied up by the time I returned from training, though, which was probably due to some type of magic.

"That was quite the performance between you two," Daphne mused from the main room while I washed up. I had dirt up crevices I hadn't even known existed after rolling around in the arena.

I laughed from inside the shower. "Not bad for just one day of training."

"Oh, that too," Daphne said nonchalantly. "You looked like you'd been training for years. But I was referring to the whole glaring at any male who looked at you and then pinning you in front of everyone. I mean, damn, girl. I knew Cole generally gave off look-at-her-too-long-and-I'll-rip-your-eyes-out vibes, but that was on another level."

"That's just how he is," I insisted while I rinsed the soap from my hair and shut the water off.

"That's how he is *with you*."

I didn't dispute the point. I toweled off and came back into the room wearing a big, fluffy robe. Daphne was at the far edge of the room, looking at the shelves that lined the far wall. Though I called it a bedroom, the place was massive. Aside from the enormous en suite bathroom complete with the walk-in shower I'd just spent twenty minutes luxuriating in, there was the giant four-poster bed and an entire living area where Daphne now stood, lined with shelves of books, an ever-burning fireplace, two comfortable seats that reminded me of those from the library that was now destroyed, and a couch that faced the flames.

"Let's get you ready." Daphne clapped her hands in excitement. "The ball starts in less than an hour, and Hecate said you're the guest of honor."

"Funny how he didn't mention it all day," I grumbled.

Daphne made a comment about thoughtless males not understanding how long it took to get properly ready, but it still bothered me. It was more than that. Why hadn't he told me? I didn't believe for a minute Cole had simply forgotten.

Daphne had already done her makeup while I was in the shower. Where she'd gotten it from, I could only imagine. Despite pestering Hecate, it was clear Daphne didn't possess a drop of magic. At least not like mine—I suspected she could've enchanted the guards to give her anything she wanted with a bit of a smile.

"Let's get you all prettied up. Not that you ever need much, lucky bitch."

Daphne liked to tease me about the fact I didn't need makeup. I had never really bothered in the pack because what difference would it make? They'd bully me mercilessly, whether my skin was clean of product or mascara was running. If anything, Sabine would've enjoyed the latter more.

But I found myself wanting to wear it. Not because I truly needed it, but I just wanted to feel pretty rather than functional.

The realization surprised me, but there it was. For the first time in my life, I actually wanted someone to look at me and think I was the most beautiful person in the room.

"He will. But I think he'd look at you that way even if you were covered in mud."

I hadn't realized I'd spoken aloud.

"I've never wanted someone like this," I confessed.

"You've never wanted anything." Daphne's voice was soft. "But you deserve it, Avery. You just have to take a chance."

She'd positioned me on the couch, the warm embers lighting my face while she began to uncap various products and apply them.

"What if it's the wrong thing to do, though?"

"What could be wrong about it?" Daphne countered. "He's hot, he's obviously into you, you're into him, and he'd rip the world apart to protect you. Goddess, Avery, if I understand Hecate right, he did do that."

"He's keeping stuff from me, Daphne. The shit about me having been reincarnated from his queen? How is that possible? And then you have Hecate saying I'm supposed to become the queen again, but she won't answer any questions either."

"Quit scrunching your eyebrows. It's messing me up," Daphne instructed. "And, Avery... does it really matter?"

I opened my mouth, but she cut me off with a look.

"Okay, yeah, it matters. I don't like the secrets either. I

don't like that everyone looks at you like they want something from you when you walk through the halls, like they're waiting for you to break into song or something when you've already given so much. All of them are keeping secrets. But that doesn't matter when it comes to what's between you and Cole. He cares about you, and I think he'd kill himself before he'd do something to hurt you." She finished applying my lipstick, my lips parted in shock as I processed what Daphne had said.

"There. Now *those* are lips he's going to fall over himself to kiss."

I blushed.

Daphne set to work on my hair, taming the drying tangle of red locks into a proper shape while the heat of the flames dried the strands.

"Do you really think it's okay to look past all of it and just... take a leap of faith? Everything in my head says it's a bad idea."

"Of course your head is going to say that. You're in Hell, and I think it's an improvement over what you went through with our pack. But forget all of that. What does your heart say, Avery?"

CHAPTER XXIX

I *LOVE HIM.*

"It says... I want him." It was as close to the truth as I could handle.

"Then *tell* him that. You've already died once, Avery." Daphne's voice was somber. "Do you want to waste a second chance by filling it with regrets?"

What would that mean if I died again and never gave Cole and me a chance? Just the thought made my stomach clench. "No."

"Then there you have it. Now, let's get you in this dress."

I hadn't doubted something would be provided to me, so I was unsurprised when I went to the closet and opened the door to find the dress.

But the dress was beyond anything I'd ever seen before, let alone worn. In my time in Moon-Ghost, I'd relied on Daphne's secondhand clothes more than anything else, living in frayed jeans and tees.

"Wow," Daphne breathed. "And I thought *my* gown was nice. Put it on!"

It took the two of us to get me in the dress and lace it up. I could barely believe my reflection.

It wasn't simply green, but a sparkling forest tone that looked as rich as the hunting grounds in spring. The material was satin with sparkling beads strategically placed to enhance my curves before fading out into the large skirt and train. The sleeves were sharp and off-shoulder, giving the dress a powerful appearance. The train laid out elegantly behind me. The color brought out the hue of my hair, finally tamed under Daphne's careful hand, and matched the ruby necklace that hung on my neck.

"You look like you should be wearing a crown," Daphne mused.

I couldn't even argue. I knew exactly what she meant.

We finished getting ready. I helped Daphne into her own gown, a sleek gray sheath that flared out at the bottom. If the ball was supposed to start an hour after training, then we were going to be fashionably late because we'd blown past that deadline.

And yet, I felt lighter than I had before.

We opened the bedroom door and there was Cole.

I'd thought I'd seen Cole looking regal before, but this was on another level. His attire was formal, almost historic looking. He wore formal pants and a military jacket with a gold chain fitted across his broad chest. Over his shoulder was a velvet cape. Gold chains held the outfit in place, secured with emerald stones on the ends. Every stitch of fabric was black, in a way that could've washed out a weaker man but just highlighted how dangerous the male in front of me was.

He'd been casually leaning against the wall, arms folded across his chest, when I'd opened the door. Once he spotted me, he moved, standing up to his full height as his gaze raked over me. It was heated and possessive as it took in every swath of fabric that had turned me from his sparring mate into a formidable woman.

Daphne excused herself to head to the ball. I barely noticed. I was transfixed.

I love this male.

"A glimpse of you would bring a lesser male to his knees."

The compliment rolled over my skin like a warm fur coat, covering me with pleasure. "Thanks. You're not half bad yourself." And there was no doubt, looking at him, that he was *not* a lesser male.

The silence stretched another beat, and I self-consciously played with the necklace at my throat.

"I thought you might want an upgrade for the evening."

He produced a large velvet box. With a flick of his fingers, he opened it.

I gasped.

I'd never been a jewelry girl. Too easy to grab someone by a necklace and choke her, and it wasn't like I had anyone in a hurry to give me anything.

But even if I'd worn a hundred necklaces, nothing could've compared to what Cole had in his hands.

The chain itself was exquisite, a collar made of small stones two inches wide, most of them clear, sparkling diamonds interspersed with green stones that flashed in the hall lights. But the centerpiece was the emerald dangling from the choker. It was so large it should've been gaudy, but the simple teardrop shape framed by a small ring of stones made the necklace elegant.

"You can't be serious."

Cole chuckled, clearly not expecting my reaction. "And why's that?"

"I can't wear that! It's too beautiful."

"It's not half as lovely as you."

"I'll definitely lose it," I protested. "Or knock some stones out."

"That's a risk I'm willing to take."

But was I? It wasn't really the necklace I was worried about, but what it meant. The clothes I could accept. I had to wear something, and it wasn't like I could get a job here and buy my own stuff. But jewelry—especially something like this—was outside the parameters of our normal dynamic.

But hadn't I just said I would listen to my heart?

"Scared, little wolf?"

For the hundredth time, I wondered if Cole could read my thoughts. But I wasn't afraid. I'd sworn not to run away again, and that included running from my feelings for Cole. "Never."

I turned my back, sweeping my hair aside so Cole could put the necklace on. I'd never known the simple act of fastening jewelry could be so erotic. His fingers brushed my collarbone as the jewels caressed my skin. My breath caught at the same moment the choker clicked into place.

I turned back to face him. Our faces were scant inches apart as I looked up, the distance shorted by the heels I wore under my dress. He looked at me through thick, dark lashes.

I opened my mouth to say something, but it was Cole who turned away first, extending an arm.

"Let's not keep our guests waiting. Shall we?"

I took his arm. He led me down a different path until we reached a split staircase. From the angle, I could just catch glimpses of the people below, all dressed in equally elegant clothing.

"I'm going to make a fool of myself, aren't I?" I muttered out of the corner of my mouth as we began to descend the first flight of stairs.

One side of his mouth quirked in amusement. "You have nothing to fear, little wolf."

We reached a platform and pivoted to the main staircase. Over a hundred pairs of eyes turned at once to face us.

"His Majesty and his consort, Lady Avery."

I cast a questioning look at Cole as we continued down.

"Consort?"

A shrug, though I sensed a hint of tension across his shoulders. "It will do. For now."

For now. Always with these hints of more to come. I decided not to let this bother me. It suited me as well as anything else. Cole led me down the staircase, the crowd parting as we arrived. Then, as we reached farther in, as if suddenly cued, the crowd engulfed us.

A dozen voices called out with felicitations and questions and requests. I stood silently while Cole handled them. I nodded politely when I was introduced, but I couldn't even begin to put names to faces.

Someone grabbed my wrist.

I spun, ready to jerk out of their grip, but it was just Daphne.

"You look like you could use a drink," she said with a grin.

I glanced at Cole. He dipped his head in answer. It wasn't that I was seeking permission, but I felt a little bad for abandoning him.

Not bad enough to decline, though.

The crowd was overwhelming. Cole was better suited to handle all of that. Daphne cleared a path for us across the ballroom. Unlike when I was with Cole, people didn't feel compelled to move out of my way. On the contrary, several courtiers kept stopping us on the way over. The compliments fell like smooth wine off their tongues, but they were meaningless. Everyone was judging me. Was I enough?

But enough for what? I wanted to ask as yet another tight-faced citizen gave me the same polite speech that only covered the most surface-level topics. How was I enjoying the kingdom? Did I care for the weather? What was my preferred type of stallion to ride?

Disentangling myself from conversation after conversation had me craving the wine Daphne set in my hand when we finally reached the refreshments table.

"Let's go over there." I tilted my glass towards a less occupied corner of the room. "I need a break from all the staring and small talk."

Daphne snorted. "We'll need to hide you in a closet or something for that because they're nowhere near done with you."

She was right, but I hoped with another glass or two of wine I might forget it.

"This is even better than the mating ceremony," she said, her eyes sparkling as she surveyed the crowd.

"Definitely," I agreed. I knew what she meant. The mating ceremony was the biggest event every year, even more so on a wolf's first year attending. Shifters in Moon-Ghost customarily dressed up like it was prom, wearing dresses and suits, picked out months in advance. You could meet your mate any year, but the first time going you had the biggest chance. Most looked forward to it for years, with parents going all out taking pictures and friends riding together.

But for me, the mating ceremony had never been anything but a beacon of freedom. For years, I'd hoped I'd find my mate and be set free of my pack.

In a way, that had come to pass.

"Sabine would lose her shit if she saw you wearing that necklace. She was so proud of that eighteen-karat necklace Jett gave her to wear to the ceremony. She bragged about it for weeks, remember?"

She'd been wearing that same golden necklace when she'd torn my intestines out, but there was no point mentioning it. Instead, I grinned at my friend, relishing how Sabine would lose her mind with jealousy. Although Daphne was the daughter of the pack Beta, Sabine had always styled herself as the pack princess and future Alpha female.

Yet now, I saw just how small the world we'd inhabited had been. There were no parties like this, no magic, nothing but dickish Alphas in power who liked to lord it over the others.

I survived her. The thought made me stand straighter.

"Who's that?" I asked, discreetly following Daphne's gaze. She kept stealing looks at one of the guards.

She blushed. "Hector. He's a guard I've run into a few times."

"Oh?" I knew my friend had been entertaining different males in her free time, but none had rated a name before.

"He's funny. You should meet him."

I smiled. "Some other time. Right now, it looks like he's dying to dance with you. You should go over there."

She glanced across the room and then back at me again. "You sure? I don't want to abandon you."

"I can fend for myself for a little while. Besides, I think I'm going to get some air anyway."

Needing no further encouragement, Daphne set off to her new beau and I went the other way to find a place that wasn't swarming with people.

The balcony I came across was blessedly empty. It wasn't large, which was probably why, maybe five feet across. It faced towards the back of the castle. In the distance was the wall that encircled the capital. I cast my gaze upward, thinking about the stars back home. In Hell, there were no stars. No sun. Just a lightening and darkening of the red sky throughout the day to signal the passage of time.

"Enjoying the view?"

CHAPTER XXX

"You!"

There, once again, was Phaidros. I had no idea where he'd come from. I hadn't heard any footsteps, nor had I seen his distinct features in the crowd. He was dressed similarly to the men in the ballroom, his outfit somewhat medieval, a splash of red standing out against his black skin. Where the sky was absent of stars, the ones etched on Phaidros's skin seemed to glow. The subtle scent of cloves coated the air.

He grinned. "Missed me, love?"

"I was stuck as a wolf for three days because of you!" Green flames sparked between my fingers.

Phaidros tensed for half a second, glancing at the power held in my palms before relaxing again, that practiced, carefree mask sliding back into place.

"Heard that was quite the palace spectacle."

I growled.

"Come on, love, we did have a deal after all. In the grand scheme, that was a rather small price for what I gave you, isn't it?"

"I don't trust you as far as I can throw you, Phaidros. And right now, I'm rather tempted to toss you off this balcony."

"You could try, love." He adjusted the lapels on his suit while leaning against the shadowed wall, then canted his head to the side. "But that will have to wait for another evening."

He flicked his wrist and a portal lit the wall behind him.

"Wait!" I wanted to ask him about the teeth I'd planted.

"Don't worry. We'll be seeing each other very soon."

Before I could lunge and grab him by those crimson lapels and shake some answers from the demon, he tipped back into the portal, which immediately shut behind him.

"Lady?"

Cole's captain of the guard, Stefan, stood in the doorway.

"Making sure I'm not running off?" I joked.

The joke bounced off Stefan like a lead ball into the ocean. "I've been tasked with keeping an eye on you, Lady Avery. It's an honor." He tacked on the last bit at the end as if to counter the boredom in his voice.

Babysitting duty was probably extremely tedious and not exactly befitting someone of his station.

"I'll go back to the party, don't worry." I pushed off the balcony railing. "Never know what riffraff is hiding in the shadows anyway." I glared at the spot where Phaidros had been.

"Riffraff?" Stefan sounded affronted. "We would *never* allow such a breach!"

There was no point in bringing up the Libra demon. Stefan escorted me down the hallway, following half a step behind me. I guess I'd accidentally given him the slip before.

"Stefan, can I ask you something? It's a bit nosy."

"Of course, Lady Avery. I will be of service any way you require."

Stefan clearly took his duty very seriously. Then again, one look at his stiff shoulders and cropped hair could've told me that.

"Why are you in Hell? Like... how did you get here? When did you die?"

The older male considered my barrage of questions. "I supposed by now it's been centuries. Like most others, I lived in the realm of the living. I was a simple warlock. When I died, I found myself here. It's hard to say why some do and some don't. It was an inhospitable place at the time, though it got better when the ruling powers were balanced. For a long time, I was aimless. Eventually, I wandered into the capital and decided to take up as a simple foot soldier. The days can get monotonous, you understand. It gave me purpose."

"Then how did you become captain?"

"May I be frank?"

"I'd prefer you be Stefan." My lame joke drew about as much laughter as a clown at a funeral. I wasn't sure why I kept trying. "I mean, of course. Please."

"After your—well, the queen's—disappearance a century

ago, the realm descended into chaos. I would never speak ill of His Majesty, but the perception was that he took the loss hard. The queen was always the compassionate side of the throne. Without one ruler and with the other distancing himself from leading the people, there was a need to organize and reign in the ensuing mayhem. I had the opportunity to prove myself and did so. Please, do not think any of what I say is a criticism—I am proud to serve the crown."

He might say that, but I sensed there was a great deal Stefan omitted in his brief explanation. But no wonder everyone kept expecting something from me. I—and it seemed I had to accept that I was—had held a significant position in their society as their queen. An advocate for the people. And then I'd disappeared, and everything went to shit.

No wonder half of them seemed to blame me. Even if few dared do so publicly out of fear of Cole's wrath.

The ballroom was still vibrating with chatter when I returned. Thankfully, no one seemed to notice my reappearance. It would be a matter of minutes until I was swarmed by different members of the court again, but for now, all I wanted was to find Cole.

Daphne was on the dance floor. Not with the male from before, who was on duty, though she kept glancing over at him in a way that told me she'd rather be in his arms. My friend was developing *quite* the crush. The expression on her face made it obvious.

I hoped I wasn't so easy to read.

Cole was in conversation with someone, but he quickly ended it, his amber eyes spotting my approach.

"Can I talk with you?"

Cole offered an upturned hand. "Come dance with me first."

"*You* dance?" Cole didn't strike me as the kind to gallivant around the dance floor.

"With you, yes." The affection in the words made me shiver.

"I'll step all over your feet. I don't know how to do all of this." I tossed a hand in the direction of all the graceful couples who navigated the dance floor with ease. Even Daphne looked graceful.

"If you can handle besting me—temporarily—in the ring, you can handle a little waltz."

"Temporarily?" I huffed, affronted. Still, I hesitated to take his hand. I'd been sort of okay tonight. Now I was going to make a fool of myself in front of Cole's entire court.

"Trust me, little wolf."

I took his hand.

Though the dance floor had been crowded, as with everything, the people parted for us as we stepped onto the floor. Self-consciousness turned my cheeks pink, but I focused on Cole. He led me through a series of easy steps, the music a comfortable waltz. I fell into the steps, following his lead.

Like with swordplay, the steps to the dance came more naturally than I would have expected.

I'd slept side by side with Cole, rolled over him in the training ring. I wouldn't pretend those acts didn't have an effect on me. But moving against him, swaying to the rhythm so that our steps and breaths were in sync, the scantest distance between us, his smoke-filled scent taunting the edges of my senses, was another experience. To everyone in the room, he was a fearsome ruler. Yet to me, he was simply Cole. An enigma and an answer rolled into one devastating male.

"What do you think?"

I tilted my head up to better look him in the eyes. "Of what?"

"Everything. The ball. The kingdom."

I considered. "It's unlike anything I've ever seen or done before. It's a touch overwhelming, but it's not bad. The people are interesting." By interesting, I meant extremely intrusive and exhausting.

He laughed. "Little liar. I suspect you find these gatherings as boring as I do."

Okay, he had me there.

"You're bored?" I challenged.

"Not anymore." He spun me abruptly, and I twirled in his arms before landing closer to him than before.

His gaze fell to my lips. Instinctively, I wetted them, looking at his own full lips and imagining the taste of them.

Do you want to waste a second chance by filling it with regrets?

"I want to ask a question and you to give me a straight answer, Cole. Just one."

Our eyes met. I hoped mine showed just how serious I was.

"Am I to be your queen?"

"You're to be whatever you want, Avery." His knuckles grazed my cheek, his other arm wrapped around my lower back. "You owe these people—and me—nothing. You have already given more than enough."

But that wasn't me, I wanted to argue. *Or was it?* I had no memory of a past life in this realm, but sometimes things would hit me—a bit of swordplay, the steps in the dance, and I knew it wasn't simply luck that let me navigate the streets of the city with unusual ease.

But my counterargument was cut short. Hecate slipped through the crowd. She looked divine, as always. Her dress was a simple cut, a single, long-flowing piece of navy linen that was clasped at the shoulders and cinched at the hips before falling to the floor.

A trickle of alarm went down my spine because Hecate looked panicked.

Hecate *never* looked panicked.

"We have a problem."

CHAPTER XXXI

H ECATE WHISKED US OUT of the ballroom. No one dared interrupt us.

"What is it?" Cole's voice was a sharp order.

Hecate spun back to us.

"It's awake."

Cole...

Cole *flinched*.

Cole, King of Hell and the most powerful male I'd ever met, actually flinched.

"What is?" I asked.

"The dragon," Hecate said quickly. "It's a sign. Something triggered it."

A sinking feeling solidified in my stomach.

"Where?" Cole asked.

"Not far. Maybe ten minutes from the city."

It would reach the unprotected villagers even sooner.

"I have to go." He turned to me. "Stay with Hecate."

"I should go with you," Hecate protested.

Cole shook his head. "I need Avery to be protected."

That wasn't going to happen. "No."

Both looked at me as if suddenly realizing I was there. "I'll go with you. Hecate can help, and I can too."

Cole looked ready to argue. He didn't like being contradicted on the best of days, but I wasn't backing down from this. After a tense second, he nodded. "Very well. We need to go now. There's no time to waste. Which direction?" He snapped up two swords from nearby guards. He tossed one scabbard in my direction and fixed the other against his waist.

"Northwest."

Cole teleported the three of us without hesitation.

It was late. The dark sky that had been so peaceful moments ago now seemed far too ominous. The wind kicked up, colliding with us as we landed on the grass. The settlements were barely half a mile away from us.

"It's been millennia," Cole hissed. "Why now?"

"You *know* why," Hecate said, voice laden with regret.

My wolf was on edge. The two of them were basically unstoppable as far as I was aware, but this had them freaked.

Cole and I drew our blades.

"I'll get its attention." Hecate's voice was strong. "I'll have one shot when it appears. You two need to take advantage and put it down."

Cole laughed, but there was no humor. "If only killing the undead was so easy. Once you distract it, get back to the city. Reinforce the barriers and ready the troops."

Hecate's response was lost to the wind. It turned from a bluster to a roar, a powerful beat thrumming over the land. An ear-splitting screech cut through the night.

And then the dragon crested over the hill.

It was the most frightening creature I'd ever seen. The creature was massive. Its wings spanned over fifty feet, its body just as long. It approached, talons outstretched, while it screeched again.

But that wasn't the truly terrifying part.

I understood exactly what they meant about it being un-dead.

The flesh of the creature was rotted in some parts and completely gone in others, revealing the empty skeleton underneath whatever scales it had. Its wings were in tatters, like torn fabric that somehow still let it soar. One eye was a violent red, the vertical pupil fixed on the three of us. The other was a hollow socket of the skull.

"Shield your eyes!"

A flash of light erupted, bright as the sun. I barely shut my eyes in time.

"Now!" Cole ordered.

We charged. The creature was flying low, having dipped from the distraction.

We needed to bring the creature to the ground, even if it was only temporary to stand a chance. Cole went left, I went right. I summoned vines, trying to grab the legs of the beast to bring it down, but the beast ripped through them after barely a second.

"The wings, Avery!"

Cole cleared the distance and leaped onto the outstretched membranous wing. I followed his lead. The dragon roared in fury, flapping its wings. I clung onto an exposed bone, trying to get enough of a grip to maneuver my blade. And then, I drove it into the exposed membrane.

The beast roared in pain, and if I wasn't fighting for my life, I might've felt bad. Cole must've done the same because suddenly the creature crashed down.

I jumped off the wing in time to avoid being crushed by the massive spikes on it.

If we thought the fight was going to be much easier now that the dragon couldn't fly, we were in trouble. It swung its wings, trying to impale us with the jagged tips. When we made the mistake of getting too close, it attempted to snap us up with its massive maw.

"How do we kill it?" I called.

"We can't!" Cole shouted back. "We can only hack it into enough pieces to stop it from moving."

Easier said than done. I tried to drive my blade into its forelegs, but the scales protecting them were as strong as iron.

"Can your magic do anything?"

"It's undead!"

Guess that meant no.

We tried to circle the creature, but it nearly knocked me out with a sweep of its rotted tail. Sparring in the room had been invigorating. This? This was life or death. If we didn't stop the dragon here, it would reach the village in no time at all. Even if the walls provided protection, there was no guarantee the settlements could be evacuated in time.

Cole and I took turns ruthlessly hacking at the legs in vain.

Adrenaline pumped through my blood, sharpening my senses. Our magic was useless here. I hadn't realized how much I'd come to trust it.

The dragon lunged for Cole. I charged at its outstretched neck, hoping to slice away part of the patchy skin. *Crack.* My blade collided with a crunch. The dragon roared in pain, rearing up on two legs. I landed on three limbs, barely keeping my grip on the blade.

The only thing that succeeded in doing was pissing off the dragon. It landed again and turned its attention fully on me. I danced back out of the way of its claws. We were getting closer and closer to the houses. Crap.

My body was exhausted. Sparring, the ball, all on too little sleep. But this was no time to rest.

The undead dragon surged forward, catching me off guard. My sword went flying. I was knocked to the ground, and this time I didn't land right. My ankle twisted at an unnatural angle.

Fuck.

The creature must've been intelligent. The look in its eyes was furious, but there was more to it.

I looked at it and I saw the pits of Tartarus.

And it saw an easy target.

This was it. There was no way I could dodge this next strike. I couldn't even stand.

The beast swiped at me with another massive claw.

It should've killed me.

But in a fraction of a second, Cole surged across the battle-field and pushed me aside. The talon sliced through his back like tissue paper, soaking the dark fabric.

My heart stopped.

Cole's amber eyes were half open, fixed on me.

"Run, Avery," he said, desperate. "Get away."

I forced myself onto my broken ankle. And I ran. I ran with everything I had to reach Cole. Pain exploded through my nerve endings, but none of it compared to the fact I couldn't breathe as I looked at Cole.

He can't be... he can't be!

I threw my body over his. The dragon had reared back and readied itself for a killing blow.

Live. Live. *Live.*

I chanted the word over and over in my head. There was no logic, no reason left in me. Just a desire to live. I wanted to live. Cole *had* to live. The citizens of Hell. Daphne. Hecate.

Life. We all deserved life.

I held onto that thought with everything I had. *And if I lose him in this life, I will find him in another.*

I've done it before.

Live. Live. Live.

I waited for the killing blow to land. For the dragon to snap us into its powerful jaws and treat us to the wonders of an undead digestive tract.

But the blow never came.

Hesitantly, I lifted my head to look while still shielding Cole's body with my own.

The dragon's mouth was just three feet from me. It was bent low, as if on the precipice of swallowing us whole when it cocked its head to the side. It was looking at me curiously. My skin was covered in a glowing green web of magic.

It was instinct that made me extend a hand to the creature that nearly killed the male I loved.

Live.

I unraveled my arm and lifted an open palm.

The dragon pressed its rotted-flesh muzzle into my hand, the nostrils flaring at the touch.

Live.

The green net of magic extended past my skin. It sparked across the undead dragon, covering it in a matter of seconds, from the tips of its horn to the edges of its wings, the broken limbs flaring out.

Live.

Flesh grew on the dragon, first filling in exposed gaps that were slowly closing with growing scales as the newly knitted tendons were hidden under the impenetrable armor. The rotted flesh mended into deep crimson scales.

A wave of exhaustion hit me, but I pushed at the thought again.

Live.

And it did. The final piece slid into place as the empty socket filled with another vertical, slitted eye that seemed to appraise me.

It was possible I had just done something very stupid. Healed the creature we'd barely managed to maim and guaranteed the deaths of everyone I cared about.

But then the dragon knelt before me. Shut its eyes and dipped its head to the ground.

Cole let out a groan under me. Frantically, I shoved off of him and checked his wound.

It was deep. So, so deep.

I had to get him back to the castle so Hecate could heal him. There was no way I could carry him.

I looked back at the fifty-foot-long dragon that had settled next to me. Its eyes snapped open.

This had better work.

CHAPTER XXXII

FLYING A DRAGON WOULD'VE been the coolest thing I'd ever done if not for the fact that the male I loved was bleeding out over its glistening, newly grown scales.

"I need to go to the castle," I'd told it, hauling Cole's broken body up onto its back. I settled us between ridges and tried to hold him steady while praying the dragon understood me. The dragon launched up with a flap of its powerful wings and steadily gained height until I could see around for miles and miles. From this angle, the realm seemed endless, its citizens nothing more than small specks in the fading light.

It drew closer and closer to the castle. *Please, let me make it in time.* I refused to consider the alternative.

The issue with approaching on a dragon that had threatened to destroy the city not half an hour ago?

Hecate had had time to rally the troops, including archers on the roof of the castle.

A hundred bows drew back, aimed at the dragon.

"Don't shoot!" I yelled over the roar of the dragon's wings. "Don't shoot!"

"Stand down!" Hecate ordered, appearing from the crowd in the same blue dress I'd seen her in before. "Clear a space for the dragon to land!"

The soldiers obeyed, and the dragon landed on the massive castle roof. I threw myself down, taking Cole with me as I rushed over to Hecate.

"You brought it back to life." The awe in Hecate's voice would've taken me aback if I wasn't so focused on Cole.

"Heal him," I begged. "He got hurt in the battle."

"I'm... fine..." Cole forced out while I held him up, one palm on his chest, the other woven between his own to support him.

"If you're fine, I'm a panther shifter," I snapped, the fear that currently squeezed at my throat doing a number on my normally immaculate bedside manner.

She appraised Cole with a quick, experienced glance. "You can heal him better than I can."

"We never learned how to do that!" I protested.

She shook her head. "You already healed yourself once. It's a natural formation of your magic. Trust yourself, Soteria."

Cole sagged in my grip. I set him down and sent a worried glance back to the enchantress.

"Concentrate on your magic. Let it find the wound and heal him," she advised. "Start by placing your hands on his body and then focus."

My magic was running on fumes after the battle, but collapsing in exhaustion wasn't an option. I shifted my attention back to Cole. His eyes were cracked, the slits of yellow barely seeing. As gently as I could, I opened up his shredded vest and set my hands on his chest. The blood had soaked the garment through. The warmth of his blood coated my fingertips. I wanted to hurl. Instead, I forced out a ragged breath and shut my eyes.

When I'd healed myself before, it had been out of necessity. It had been imperative I rescue Daphne from the Moon-Ghost pack cells.

Now, I had to save Cole. Letting him die was not an option.

I focused on my memories of Cole, trying to guide my magic to him. To push it into him. Memories of training with him. *His smirk when he teased me. His eyes when they were filled with silent laughter. The protective way he'd murdered countless foes to keep me safe. The way he drove me crazy when training, even though it was all in service to keep me safe. The way he'd held his arm out for me to escort me to the ball. The brush of his fingers on my neck when I was half-asleep. The hundred times he'd appeared in my dreams, my only constant comfort in a ruthless pack. The way he made me want to live life to the fullest, not just accept whatever happened, but to stand up and fight.* Just as I would fight this injury and bring him back to me.

As I pushed the memories, the magic, into him, something ricocheted back into me. A bridge between us opened.

Images and foreign emotions assailed me. *Me, across a thousand dreams over the years. The fury when I confided how my packmates mistreated me. The sorrow when I confidently declared I would find my moon-matched mate. The lust that roared through him when he pleasured me, tinged with resignation that it could only be a dream. The surprise at finding me in his bedroom. The way I looked in his clothes. The time he'd given me ugly clothes in a fruitless effort to tamp down his desire for me. The amusement that tickled him when we bantered back and forth in training. Pride when I'd defeated the Leo demon. Bone-freezing fear when I'd been petrified. A mix of anger, respect, and fear when I'd poisoned him and escaped the realm. A thousand emotions that constantly warred within him—a ruthless need to tear anyone who wronged me limb from limb and a desire that burned brighter than I ever could've imagined.* A kaleidoscope of images flashed through my mind—*my hair wet from the shower, my skin slick with sweat from training, my content smile as I curled into a chair in the library to read, unaware that he watched me from the shadows. My wolf running through the woods. My fingers sparking with power. My eyes pleading for him to take me, to claim me, in the woods.*

And beneath it all was an emotion far, far stronger than any of those. To call it love was an insult. Experiencing it secondhand was like drowning in a raindrop.

"You saved the king," Hecate said, snapping the telepathic

link between Cole and me. "You've saved us all, Avery."

I jerked back. There was Cole, amber eyes open and fixed on my own. At once, it was obvious that the bridge between us had gone both ways.

For a moment, it was only the two of us.

Then, a movement in the periphery caught my attention. I stood as I turned, Cole rising by my side with ease, as if he'd never been injured.

A hundred soldiers faced me, and at Hecate's declaration, as one, they knelt.

"Soteria," Hecate called out, but not to me.

The soldiers echoed, facing me, still kneeling. "Soteria." Then again. "Soteria! Soteria! Soteria!"

I stepped back, stunned, and knocked into Cole.

"What does it mean?" I asked him softly.

His eyes glowed with pride. "It means 'savior.'"

W E EVENTUALLY BROKE AWAY from the throng of soldiers. Hecate could handle the aftermath. The dragon had flown off, and no one seemed worried, so I took that as a positive sign.

It was a good thing too, because I was about a hairsbreadth from passing out on the roof.

It was impossible to look at Cole the same way since I'd

healed him. The flood of emotions was a heady mix. Was it really possible he could feel the same way? The never-ending desire, the craving, the *need*... He walked now, unconcerned that his shirt was torn to shreds and dried blood had crusted around every inch of exposed skin. I hadn't seen a mirror, but I wasn't much better. Yet even now, he looked perfect. Or even better, like battle-honed Cole was his natural state. The tattoo wrapped around his back was on full display, and I wanted to wipe away the blood that marred its edges.

"If you keep looking at me like that, I'll take you against the wall and make you scream loud enough for the entire castle to hear," Cole said casually, without turning to face me.

I flushed, suddenly not feeling tired at all.

"Just let me wash off the blood first," I said. It was meant to come out as a joke.

But as Cole shut the doors to our bedroom behind us, I realized how much I meant it. Not just that I didn't want to have sex while covered in Cole's blood. I wanted to have Cole in every way possible. I wanted to be screaming his name and digging my claws into his skin and to claim him in truth the way he'd claimed my heart.

Through unspoken agreement, we went into the shower together. Our tattered clothes fell to the ground until we were bare under the hot spray.

The water ran red with blood.

Cole produced a bar of soap and silently began to run it

over my body. Once my face was clean, his tender caress continued down my arms. I faced away from him as he cleaned my back. The bar trailed lower. My thighs. My calves.

When he turned me to face him, the simple touches grew slower.

I wanted to savor the touch, but instead, I looked at the flawless male in front of me and shook.

Once I started, I couldn't stop.

The bar paused on my collarbone.

"Talk to me, little wolf."

I swallowed. "I thought I was going to lose you." I looked at the shower floor, the white tile stained pink from the trickle of blood that fell off both of us. "And when I thought that... it was unbearable. It was the worst moment in my existence. But the absolute cruelest part was that you could have died without me ever being honest about how I felt. And that would've been the most vomit-inducing part of it all, that I never gave us a chance."

He curved a finger and tilted me up to face him.

"Cole, I don't know what quirk of destiny let me find my way to you, but I've never wanted anyone the way I want you. It's more than that. *I love you.* And I don't want to have a single regret."

The soap clattered to the floor as Cole suddenly wrapped both arms around me and pulled my naked body against his own.

The shower water was hot, but Cole was warm. A tender warmth that I wrapped my hands around while I still shook. It must've been the shock of the battle finally wearing off. Tears pricked at my eyes, the spray of the shower hiding them as I tucked my head into his chest.

"I won't let you have a single regret, Avery," he vowed. "You are my heart and my soul, or whatever black pit sits in my chest."

When the shaking abated, Cole moved, pressing my back against the tiled wall. And then he slid down in front of me, falling to his knees as he continued to look up at me with dominant eyes.

"I'm forever in awe of you, little wolf. You have *no idea* how incredible you are. How irresistible you are. How *mine* you are."

I shivered at his possessive words.

"But I'm going to show you."

That was all the warning Cole gave before pressing his face between my legs.

And then he licked.

I gasped at the contact.

He licked again, running the length of my slit. He did it slowly, like he was savoring the taste.

My fingers threaded through his wet, black hair as I pulled him closer. Cole continued his languid feasting, my body arching at the contact as my arousal grew. I widened my stance, trying to guide him where I needed him.

"More," I demanded.

Cole pulled away. "I don't intend to rush a single moment of tonight, little wolf. Prepare yourself."

It was the sweetest torture. When Cole finally dipped his tongue inside my entrance, I moaned. He was a master at his craft, and no matter how I tugged or ordered him, he refused to speed up his pace.

He held my hips firmly between his large hands, the callouses a rough caress. He ate me out like it felt as good for him as it did for me. His tongue lifted from my center to tease at my clit. He sucked, nipped, and tortured me until I was gasping for breath.

"Are you going to make me beg?" I complained when, for the third time, he brought me to the edge only to take it away.

"Only because you like to," Cole said, barely pausing before he returned to his teasing.

"I don't." My strong protest was undercut by a moan.

"I can change your mind."

Cocky bastard! "I'll just finish myself if you won't."

I lowered a hand to my clit, determined to get the relief I craved.

Or tried. The second my hand came within reach of it, Cole let out a growl and pinned my wrist to the tiled wall. The other hand met the same fate. He looked up at me, yellow eyes flashing in challenge.

"You'll come when I say so, little wolf, and not a moment before."

I shivered again. There was no one else I would tolerate this from.

Yet the raw dominance contained in Cole's words was a potent aphrodisiac.

"You're not going to leave me on the edge again, are you?" I hissed, recalling our dream encounter months ago. Dream Cole had used the same method of torture. Of course, at the time, I hadn't realized it had really been Cole.

"I might." Cole laughed against my thighs, enjoying having me at his mercy. "But since you saved my life, I suppose I can be magnanimous."

He returned to the task with renewed vigor, and I almost lost my footing. "I'll keep that in mind." *Save the King of Hell and get your rocks off with him. Solid trade.*

He kissed me like a dying man and I was his only chance at salvation. My moans grew more frenzied, my orgasm building and building.

I said I wouldn't beg.

I lied.

"Please," I cried. "Please, please, please. *Don't stop.*"

And then, finally, he granted my request. My orgasm slammed through me, an electric sensation that turned my whole body into a supernova. Cole didn't let up, making me ride the wave of pleasure out over and over while he continued to suck and lick and slam me over the edge.

I slumped against the wall.

Cole lifted me easily, shutting the water off as he carried me out of the bathroom. He tucked me against his chest, a brief reprieve. The warmth of the hearth filled the room, the flames the only light in the space.

That was fine. My male was meant to be looked at in firelight.

He set me down, the heat from the fireplace drying our still-soaked figures.

I might have come, but our evening was far from done. We stood for a moment. I inspected the male in front of me the same way he looked at me. My Alpha. *My King.*

While I might have found release, Cole had had no such pleasure.

Something I intended to fix.

I might have been a virgin, but I'd be damned if I was going to get a reputation for being a selfish lover.

I pushed Cole back onto the couch and then sank to my knees in front of the male. My face level with the hard erection that had pressed against me so many mornings, a tease for my dreams to chase down. He was *large*. I didn't exactly have a lot of frames of reference, but even with my shifter healing, I'd be walking bow-legged tomorrow if that thing went inside me.

Who was I kidding? There was no *if. No regrets,* he'd

promised. And going one more night without knowing every inch of Cole would be an unforgivable mistake.

"You don't have to," he said, his voice roughened by lust.

"Just try and stop me."

I grasped his erection in my hand. It seemed to dwarf it, my fingers unable to even fully wrap around it. A bead of precum appeared at the tip.

Mine.

I dipped my tongue to it on instinct. To sample his salty taste. His cock jerked at the contact, and Cole, normally un-flappable Cole, gasped.

I clenched my legs at the sound. More. I wanted more. I wanted to devour him. I didn't know exactly what I was doing, but enthusiasm had to count for something, right? Maybe like swordplay or dancing, I'd magically be good at it.

And if not... well, Cole was nothing if not a diligent teacher.

I licked his length, teasing him the way he did me. His scent coated my tongue and I moaned in delight.

"Fuck. Your tongue."

I arched at the praise. I kissed the head of his cock, want-ing more of his delicious taste on my tongue. Tentatively, I opened my mouth and took the tip between my lips. Cole bucked at the contact. My Alpha's control was fracturing.

I wanted it to shatter.

I took more of him. It was a strange sensation. But I loved

his reaction. His hands grabbed fistfuls of hair. He didn't push me down but held me against him. The possessive act turned me on, encouraging me to take more of him.

"That's it, good girl. Take me deeper."

I moaned at the praise, and Cole's answering groan at the vibrations was the most erotic sound I'd heard in my entire life.

"Gonna make me spend on your pretty little tongue."

I went faster, encouraging him. I wanted to make Cole come. I wanted to taste him, to swallow him whole.

"Yes. Faster!" he ordered.

I was eager to obey, moving up and down at a punishing rate, my hand following the slick length while my other teased my own entrance. Sucking Cole off was seriously turning me on.

"Fuck!" Cole came with a cry. A spray of salty yet tasty liquid hit my tongue, and I swallowed without hesitation. Cole panted, leaning back on the couch. I braced my hands on his knees, looking up so I could survey the effect I'd had on the most powerful male in the realm. It was a power of its own to give pleasure like this. I could understand why he'd like to draw it out.

He looked at me with something like awe.

"Incredible."

I grinned up at him. "Not bad for a first time."

"It's good it was your first time." He stroked my hair. "If

you'd done that to another male, I'd be forced to rip his throat out."

He didn't sound like he was joking. I decided to take the possessive remark as a compliment.

His erection had temporarily gone down, but it was once again curving up in invitation. "Isn't that thing supposed to, like, deflate?" I asked.

Cole chuckled. "Oh, I'm not letting you off that easily, little wolf."

I should've been sated after the shower.

Not even close.

Cole pulled me onto the couch, breathing in my scent like he needed it to survive. I straddled him, his erection resting between the cleft of my legs. The contact made me moan. I undulated back and forth, coating him with my wetness.

"I'm going to take you, little wolf. Last chance to back away. We can still stop." The words were gentle even as Cole's muscles strained to restrain his movement.

"Don't hold back."

That was the only permission Cole needed.

He flipped me over. I looked up at him, his black locks falling forward, his eyes dark as he looked at me through his lashes. He was as glorious as he'd been in my dreams.

"Be careful what you wish for."

"Make me."

Cole nipped my earlobe for my insolence. I arched at the

contact, the edge of pain heightening my pleasure. He didn't break eye contact as he adjusted himself, pressing against my entrance. The head teased the opening, and I gasped. I was suddenly, not entirely irrationally, worried that it might not fit.

"You're going to take all of me," Cole ordered.

I wanted to bark back that I didn't take commands very well, but at that moment, he began to press in more fully. My breath hitched at the contact. It wasn't exactly a comfortable feeling. Not bad, but foreign.

In more, then out a little before thrusting in again. I yelped slightly.

Cole froze in place. "You okay?"

I nodded, trying to process the overwhelming sensation. "Just need a minute to adjust."

"You're doing so good for me, little wolf." He ran a hand down the side of my face.

I arched at his words and he eased farther in.

Slowly, my body adjusted to his size. When he was finally inside me, I'd never felt so full in my life. Never so close to someone else.

"That's my girl," he praised.

I couldn't quite manage to answer, because at that moment, Cole began to move.

Cole gave me just enough time to catch my breath before he moved in and out. His cock pressed at my inner walls, stretching me to the very max. Where the sensation first felt strange, now all it left was pleasure in its wake. I didn't mask my sounds of pleasure. Cole groaned as he moved, his words never faltering in their praise while he built up to a steady rhythm, burying himself inside me over and over again.

I'd thought I was done coming after the shower, but what had transpired before was only the prelude to the main event. It was like all the pleasure before had simply whetted my appetite and now I was starving for this male. For his cock, for his words, for his scent. I wanted to possess all of him. And I wanted him to claim every part of me.

"Harder," I pleaded, needing more.

"Such a good girl. Take my cock deep," he demanded.

I had no choice but to obey.

Bliss danced at the edge of my senses. I was close, so close again, and hungry for release like I'd never been before.

"You're going to make me spend again, little wolf."

"Yes," I moaned. "More."

"Going to take my seed inside you?"

I nodded. I needed him. Every single part of him.

"I'm close, Cole," I whimpered, begging him to give me what I needed.

"Then come when I do." He grunted, thrusting faster and faster, hitting that perfect spot. "Now!"

On his command, I came. I cried out loudly, not caring if the entire castle heard. My climax was the most potent yet, sending me to dizzying heights while every nerve ending of my body was alight with pleasure. Cole came with a long, low groan that had me contracting my inner muscles to hold him in. His hot seed filled me. He pulled out and replaced his cock with his fingers, coating my insides with his come. The act was dirty as sin and it made me crave more.

I collapsed onto the couch in exhaustion. Cole lifted my boneless form over to the bed, then disappeared. I whined at the loss, but he returned barely a minute later with a hot cloth and cleaned my thighs. I'd become entirely slick with my own arousal. The gesture was tender and somehow utterly intimate. Washcloth discarded, he joined me in bed, tugging me up against him.

I rested my head on his shoulder, cherishing the contact.

"Wow," I murmured.

For a moment, the two of us just breathed. The universe was just our two chests, rising and falling as one.

"I have lived uncountable moments in agony thinking I would never see you again."

I twisted to better see Cole. His gaze was distant for a beat before he turned his head to meet my own.

"The night you walked in my dreams, I convinced myself it was an accident, a hallucination. When it happened again, I thought I could find closure in knowing somewhere you lived, even if I could never be with you." He toyed with my hair, as if still lost in thought. "When you showed up in my castle, I was once again struck. Fear and desire warred within me in equal measures. I should have sent you away for your own safety because being with me leads only to death. Yet I find you are the one thing I can never give up, Avery."

For a moment, his confession turned pained. There were still centuries of Cole I didn't understand, but this male in bed with me, I knew him as well as I knew my own heart.

"If I only ever have one more night with you, I want to spend it without a single regret."

I moved atop Cole, straddling him while I bent down to kiss him. He tasted like smoke and danger. He tasted like home. "Then let's make certain there aren't any."

Cole made certain, again and again, as he made love to me throughout the night. It was like he was etching his love into every inch of my body. I only hoped I had carved myself into his soul the way he had mine.

CHAPTER XXXIII

T HE NEXT MORNING WOULD go down as one of the best in my life. I woke with a soreness in my muscles that felt like a reward. Cole and I were intertwined in a tangle of limbs and sheets. It had been early, barely dawn when we woke, but we didn't leave the bed for hours. We showered and wound up back in bed for another hour before finally rousing ourselves. It was easy to forget within that room, but the city had nearly been destroyed by an undead dragon only hours ago. They'd be looking to their leader, which meant I was forced to share Cole with the world.

Not that he agreed.

"It can wait. Nothing matters except you," he rasped while attempting to seduce me away from the clothes I was trying to put on for a third time.

"Hecate will just *love* to hear that."

"I find I don't give a damn what that witch thinks." He nipped at my ear to prove my point. I bit down on a moan.

No. We have to be responsible. "Be good." I tried to be stern. "Go do your kingly duties, and then we can go back to canoodling after."

"My little Alpha."

I frowned. "I'm not an Alpha."

He barked a laugh. "You argue with me for sport and constantly attempt to overpower me when sparring. You're the most powerful female in the realm and a fearless protector of your friends. And just now, you attempted to order me about. If you're not an Alpha, no one is."

I barely had time to process his words before he captured my lips in another kiss. I raked my nails down his chest, wanting to anchor myself against him. Desire warred with logic, but this time, I forced myself to pull away.

Cole heaved a heavy sigh. "As you wish."

Cole went off to do whatever the King of Hell does after an undead dragon attempts to raze his kingdom. Me? The twenty-one-year-old shifter who just had sex for the first time, and not just sex, but toe-curling, six-orgasm sex?

I went off to find my best friend.

The hallways were bustling with people. Each person I saw bowed when they spotted me, and not just a slight head nod. Deep bows that made me want to scurry past.

I held back only so I could turn Cole's words over in my head while looking for Daphne.

Avery Ward. Alpha.

It didn't exactly fit, but I didn't feel like an Omega anymore either.

How things changed.

Daphne found me first, nearly barreling into me when she spotted me. She dragged me into a nearby room and shooed out the occupants, who had already begun the bowing and scraping routine.

"Can you believe this?" I jerked my head to the recently shut door.

"*Believe it?* Avery, you don't get it. All anyone has been able to talk about is how the apocalypse was coming and you somehow saved them and healed their beloved dictator—I mean, king—from certain death."

My anxiety spiked at just the mention of Cole's weak form. "Hecate could've healed him." I kept telling myself it had just been a messed-up lesson and she would've stepped in if anything had been really wrong.

Daphne shook her head. "No. Hecate said you'd already brought him back from the brink before getting to the castle. If you hadn't..."

Live, I had chanted over and over. It had turned the undead dragon alive again. Yet I'd been focused on Cole. He'd still been in terrible shape once I'd gotten to the castle. Had my magic really saved him, even then?

"You're a hero to these people, girl. Hector said that the undead dragon hadn't been seen for thousands and thousands of years, since before Cole was even the king. It showing up is a seriously bad sign. They're trying to figure out what might've caused it. It was supposed to be sealed deep, deep in Tartarus, but somehow it was able to break through." She hesitated. "In fact, I had a thought."

Ice went down my spine. *It can't be.* "It has to be a coincidence."

Daphne gave me a skeptical look but dropped the subject. She tasted the air and stared at me.

I grinned.

"You didn't."

"I did."

Daphne shrieked in delight. "Damn, girl, you act fast! How did you even have time for that between the ball and fighting a dragon?"

"Let's just say there wasn't a lot of sleeping last night," I said coyly.

"Details, bitch. I want details. If I still have my V-card, the least you can do is give me the play-by-play."

"Really? I thought you and Hector…"

Daphne glanced away. "It's weird for me, being the only living person in the land of death." Sadness tinged her words, but she shook it off. "Don't change the topic. I want to know *everything*. How was it? Was it amazing?"

I bobbed my head up and down like a dropped bobblehead. "It was better. He just… ugh. Words won't even describe it."

"Well, you better try," Daphne informed me snippily.

I did, leaving out the most intimate details. It felt good to have simple girl talk with my best friend, rather than the severe topics that normally followed us around. She gasped when I told her how we started in the shower and high-fived me when I told her about the multiple orgasm thing. It was almost enough to make me drown out the growing sense things were about to get a lot worse.

Daphne filled in the other blanks. The dragon had flown off after dropping Cole and me on the castle roof, and no one had spotted it since. The settlements had been moved into the castle in the meantime, though. They had followed my evacuation plan and not a moment too soon. It explained why the hallways were even busier than usual.

Am I to be your queen?

I'd asked Cole that before everything had gone to shit. He hadn't *really* answered. Maybe he didn't want me to be his queen again, no matter how compatible we were in the bedroom. Last time, things had gone so badly that people still held a grudge. Hopefully, the whole "fighting off the undead dragon" would do some good for my PR, but that might not change Cole's mind.

My stomach growled and I let Daphne know I was going to look for food. She offered to join, but I needed some time to myself to process.

Call it instinct, but as I passed an uncharacteristically empty hallway, my hackles rose.

When I tasted the faintest hint of cloves on my tongue, I *knew*.

"Hello, lo—"

I slammed Phaidros into the wall.

CHAPTER XXXIV

M Y HAND WRAPPED AROUND Phaidros's neck and I squeezed, pressing him into the granite. He was bigger than me, but he hadn't been expecting me to detect him so easily. I bared my teeth at the night-skinned demon. His surprise and fear tasted like ambrosia.

I was afraid. And fear no longer cowed me—it just made me angry. Because if I was right, Phaidros was even more dangerous than I'd suspected.

"You have some explaining to do." I barely recognized the feral sound as my own voice.

Ssk!

Phaidros drew his blade, pressing it against my chin.

My hands sparked in response while I grabbed his wrist. He flinched but held the blade steady.

I can't get answers if he's dead.

I released my choke hold just slightly. "If I let you go, do you promise not to portal off at the first sign of trouble?"

Phaidros nodded.

"Swear it on the Styx."

"I... swear... on the Styx."

I relaxed my hand and pulled my arm back. Phaidros recovered in a blink, sheathing his sword and adjusting his wrinkled vest in the span of two seconds.

"The teeth. Did they have anything to do with that thing?"

"That thing?" Phaidros laughed. "The undead dragon you managed to bring back to life, allowing you to regain the favor of the realm? *That* thing?"

I growled.

He shrugged as if he wasn't fazed by my theatrics now that I didn't have him pinned against the wall.

It made me want to turn furry and rip out his throat.

"Yes. I'm impressed you put it together, love. Or should I say Soteria? They seem to be singing your praises rather thoroughly."

"I'm not your love," I hissed. "How could you release that beast on us? It was supposed to be a small favor where no one got hurt. Cole nearly *died*."

"Us?" Phaidros chuckled. "I would hardly call gardening a dangerous task. Having a magical entity such as yourself plant dragon's teeth may have had a few consequences, but that wasn't part of the favor. If the dragon hadn't shown up, we'd have been square."

"Why?" I demanded. *Why would he want to bring that monstrous creature here?*

"Why, indeed. Unfortunately, *that* information isn't for

sale. And you already have a debt you need to pay on. I've come to collect."

"I won't do it. I don't care if it makes me an oathbreaker."

Phaidros's eyes flashed. "Ah, love. If only it was so easy to double-cross. But the magic binds you, as you well know since you just used it on me. There is no *oathbreaking* when it comes to the Styx."

Fear gripped me.

He can't collect if he's dead.

I launched myself at him, but Phaidros was fast. Faster than me, faster than even Cole. He used my momentum against me and pinned me to the wall, face forward. I jerked my neck aside to look at him out of my periphery. He pressed me into the cold stone, the unnatural angle painful.

He *tsked*. I had overpowered him before with the element of surprise. But now, I couldn't so much as shift in his grasp. My hands were shoved through the stone into small portals that held them like handcuffs while the sparkling yellow rings shrank around them. I couldn't call on my magic like this. *He's been hiding his true power.*

"Now, now, no need for that. You're going to keep your word to me, Avery. Or I'm going to portal out of here and find that pretty little friend of yours and kill her. Now, hush. None of that," he said with a put-out sigh as I growled at him and tried to kick him. "One more little favor and we're square. Doesn't that sound nice? Here's what you have to do:

the enchantress has a special scrying mirror in her chambers. You can identify it by the waxing and waning moons on the handle. All you need to do is take a little peek at the Alpha of your old pack for a few minutes. What's his name, Jameson? Jared?"

"Jett," I said through gritted teeth.

Phaidros snapped his fingers. "That's it. Jett. Sounds like a right prick, doesn't he?" He didn't wait for my agreement. "Just scry on Jett in the Many Moon Mirror for a few moments and your debt shall be paid."

"How do you know all of this?" How could he even know who Jett was?

"As I said, I'm not your ordinary demon," Phaidros demurred, sounding far too casual for someone who had me immobilized.

"Why, then? If I have to do it anyway, just tell me the cost."

He chuckled, looking genuinely amused at my request. "Ah, but where would the fun be in that, love?"

He eased back a fraction. I tested my hands, but they were still stuck in the wall.

"One last thing before I go. You're not to reveal this task or anything about my visit today to anyone. Not by word or deed. Wouldn't want anyone interfering with you keeping your word. You have until midnight tonight." He leaned in to whisper in my ear. "Otherwise, I'll be paying little Daphne a visit."

CHAPTER XXXV

PHAIDROS VANISHED AS SUDDENLY as he'd appeared, the scent of cloves disappearing with him.

I shook against the wall. *No good will come of this.*

I wanted to seek out Cole and immediately tell him about the stupid deal I'd made. I'd never thought I'd be back in Hell for the demon to collect, and I'd had no other way to save Daphne.

My feet refused to move.

The curse must've sensed my goal and it would stop me from doing anything that might let the others know what was going on.

Bile rose in my throat.

How had this day gone so wrong? It had started off perfectly, and now, I had to sneak into the dwellings of a powerful witch who trusted me and do something that would probably summon a swarm of undead dragons or worse. The teeth had seemed harmless. Looking in an enchanted mirror?

That had trouble spray-painted all over it.

Part of me hoped it was a sick, twisted joke Phaidros had

come up with to shove my moon-matched mate in my face. Cruel, petty, but not dangerous.

Yeah. Those supernatural manacles had "prank" written all over them.

I didn't dare delay. If Phaidros went after Daphne, I wasn't sure I'd be able to protect her, . And it wasn't like I could ask for reinforcements since, per his instructions, I was to not let anyone know anything about what had happened.

Find the mirror. Scry for a minute. Then get out. Hopefully, with the favor fulfilled, I could rush to Cole and Hecate and figure out how to fix things.

Hecate stayed in the east wing, a floor below our own on the opposite side of Cole's chambers. Though I hadn't stepped foot in her rooms, they were easy to find. The air by them was full of flowers and herbs, just like her castle garden.

Yet two familiar scents were also present. Hope leaped through my chest. The scents led to a closed door. An office?

Cole's irritated voice was at once familiar, as well as the soft, lilting tones of the witch.

If I could just open the door...

But my feet refused to go any further. I was frozen outside the door, trying to overpower the conditions Phaidros had shackled me with. I couldn't even howl in frustration.

I should just go and get this over with as soon as possible. Keep Daphne safe. Yet just as I convinced myself to do that, I caught the thread of conversation and stilled.

"The price cannot be avoided forever, Hades. She took a *life*." Hecate's voice was soft, but not as unconcerned as she normally constructed it.

Did she mean me? A life? *Maddox's life?* But why did that matter?

"You shielded the realm. They won't find her." Cole's voice was confident.

"Undead things are waking up. You *know* this. You know the consequences."

Cole growled, the animal that lurked under his skin creeping into his voice. "I know the *consequences* better than anyone."

Hecate was ever unflappable. "There must be balance, King."

"Balance?" Cole scoffed, a bitter note in the word. "What *balance* has there been for the past century?"

Hecate's voice softened. "I know you suffered. But the realm suffered too. We cannot exist without our queen any longer."

"I won't force her. She deserves peace, witch. You know this."

"I know this realm will not survive without her, and our time is growing shorter and shorter. Blazes, Hades, do you not realize what would've happened if she hadn't stopped the dragon? I'm shielding her as best I can, but it's not perfect. If anything tampers with the seal..."

What did they mean? The dragon was only the beginning? Cole and I had barely survived it. If there were more on the way, we were in trouble.

"It will last." A pause. "I will *not* allow her to be taken again."

For the hundredth time, I wished I knew what had happened. The people of Hell believed I—the former queen—had abandoned them. Yet the pain in Cole's voice was unmistakable. *Taken?*

"I pray you will have that choice," Hecate replied. "Last time, she made it for you."

The topic was dropped, and the two shifted the conversation to more stately matters. I didn't have time to waste. I moved from my listening spot and moved farther into Hecate's chambers.

Sneaking through her space felt wrong. It was a betrayal.

At least I didn't have to kiss her to do it.

The structure was unlike anything else I'd come across in the palace. The rooms were winding without rhyme or reason. A door would as easily open to a small cleaning cabinet as an impossibly large empty room or even a stone wall. One room held a green bubbling cauldron that seemed almost stereotypical. But no mirror.

The items that dotted the hall were old. The underworld in general had a mix of ages, which I supposed made sense. People died all the time. Some had been here for centuries, like Stefan, while I was a newcomer. And Hecate... Cole had never told me how old Hecate was exactly, but she might've been the oldest creature in the kingdom.

Hecate's bedroom was obvious once I reached it. Instead of wood, a door of carefully carved gold opened into a medium-sized room. The space was immaculate, though a gut feeling said it was maintained by enchantment rather than any servant being allowed in to tidy up. Purple swaths of fabric were draped over every wall, varying shades overlapping over every inch.

The air seemed to drip with magic. As if simply by sleeping in the room, Hecate's magic had permeated every stone and piece of furniture.

I stiffened, walking into the room.

I'd felt bad for trespassing through the other rooms. Yet now, the wrongness of my violation was a physical sensation. As if the very space could sense I was an intruder and wanted to shove me out.

Instinct told me the Many Moon Mirror would be here. I hadn't come across any other obvious scrying tools throughout the other rooms.

I walked farther into the room. My stomach clenched at what I was about to do. But Daphne's life was on the line. The stupid bargain I'd made wouldn't compel me forward even if I'd had a choice.

Just find it, scry, and get out. And pray the completion of

the bargain would free me to run and tell Hecate and Cole what I'd done.

The mirror wasn't present on any obvious surface. I opened desk drawers and checked under her pillow. Nothing. My search grew more desperate. If it wasn't here, I was in trouble. There were too many rooms for me to search for all of them before Phaidros's midnight deadline.

Think, Avery. Where would she hide a super-powerful mirror?

I scanned the room, hoping an idea would spark.

Then it became obvious.

Hecate wouldn't leave out the Many Moon Mirror. She was the most powerful enchantress in the realm. She'd use her magic to tuck it away somewhere.

How was I going to out-magic my teacher? I'd finally tapped into some of my base power of life, but that was no counter to Hecate's enchanting.

The first thing was just to try and find it. I shut my eyes and concentrated. The entire room was dripping in magic, more so than anywhere else. What if it was more than the fact Hecate lived here? What if it was meant to camouflage a blatant use of magic, like a spell?

The magic was not evenly dispersed throughout the room. It thickened and thinned in patches. My steps were light as I circled the room, trying to pick up on the heaviest concentration.

The vanity. I sat in the seat and ran my hands over the wood, trying to find something further out of the ordinary.

The mirror attached was large and obviously didn't match the demon's description. The glass reflected my disheveled appearance. Still, magic pulsed in the air.

Where better for Hecate to hide the mirror than within another mirror?

I rested my hands on the glass and pushed. The glass didn't give.

But my hands left no fingerprints behind either.

There was no reason to be so sure, but pure instinct said I was correct. The Moon Magic Mirror was within this one.

Getting it out wouldn't be easy. I was sorely outclassed.

But I was desperate. I rested my palm on the glass and concentrated. The magic was a lock. I needed a key. I couldn't brute force it open, that much was obvious. Just the thought of snatching the mirror sent sparks into my palm. I jerked back, then returned my hand and focused.

Hecate wouldn't want anyone stealing the mirror.

But I didn't want to *steal* the mirror. Could the magical lock sense intent? I pushed the thought forward. The image of the gold-handled mirror in my palm, in quick succession with another image of me pushing it back into its hiding place.

My hand moved forward half an inch.

Into the glass.

It's working.

I continued to craft the image in my head. *I don't want to take it. I'll give it back right away,* I promised the spell.

My hand went further and touched something. My fingers wrapped around a piece of metal, invisible behind my reflection. I pulled back.

And there, in my hand, was the exact mirror Phaidros had described. The glass was small, no more than eight inches tall and maybe five wide. The gold frame around it was ornate.

The strangest part was the glass didn't reflect anything back. It was like a piece of shiny metal.

The room itself seemed to warp now that the mirror was out of its cage. The magic was no longer simply present. It was alive. The mirror I held was more magic than a physical item. It was like holding a storm cloud.

It was exhilarating.

And yet somehow, it felt wrong in an almost crippling way.

I struggled to recall Hecate's lessons. We'd been focused on that ancient tree and life and vines. Scrying had been forbidden. Hecate hadn't put so much as a reflective surface in front of me since I'd been back.

I'd only looked in on two people before in my lessons, Cole and Daphne. Cole, who had sensed me.

Jett won't know. Cole was the King of Hell, so it made sense he was powerful enough to detect the presence of a spell. But Jett was a simple, mortal male. He was nothing I should fear, not anymore. Not even if he'd almost killed me in our last encounter.

The smallest part of me was almost curious to see my old tormentor. I had nothing to fear. Just one look and I could put the mirror back.

I tapped into my memories of the Alpha Heir. Or perhaps he was the Moon-Ghost Alpha now. Even now, I could remember his scent more intimately than I wanted. That was the curse of having your fated mate also be your tormentor for years. As much as I erased the snake from my mind, he could return with the slightest provocation.

I thought of his scent. Rivers and iron and arrogance. The curve of his jaw as he smirked at the weak Omega. The sardonic tilt of his mocking laughter.

The mirror in my hand rippled and changed.

And there he was, the silver prince. The view was from the back of his head, white-blond hair slick against his skull. I didn't recognize the room he was in. It looked almost like the throne room Cole used in the palace. My brow creased in confusion. Was there really a place like that on Moon-Ghost pack lands? Then again, I hadn't seen the dungeon until I scried on Daphne.

Just the memory of my friend, caged and weak at the hands of these Alpha pricks, sent sparks of my magic in the air.

Jett turned. He didn't realize it, but we were face-to-face. My stomach twisted. My lip curled back in an involuntary snarl.

I should put the mirror down now. I'd fulfilled the bargain. It was time to go.

I began to lower my arm when he spoke. And the words froze my blood.

"Hello, my wayward mate."

CHAPTER XXXVI

I NEARLY DROPPED THE mirror in shock.

He can see me.

No, upon further inspection, Jett wasn't looking back at me. But he must've been able to sense that I was looking in.

A shiver of frost went down my spine.

"I was wondering when that demon was going to hold up his end of the deal," Jett said, a satisfied smirk spreading over his lips. It was the smile he'd make ripping out my throat, given a chance. "The Moon Goddess will be pleased."

I slammed the mirror down on the table, severing the connection. The demon... *Phaidros had made a deal with* Jett? There was even more going on than I'd guessed. I lifted the Moon Magic Mirror against its hiding place. It sank into the glass as if the mirror was made of honey, the large pane rippling as it reclaimed the magic object.

Immediately, the room began to violently shake.

Was it the spell? No, it was bigger than this. The entire castle was shaking. Furniture came away from the walls, toppling. I didn't hesitate. I sprinted out of the room, dodging debris on my way. I ran and ran, trying to escape the labyrinth of Hecate's chambers. Neither she nor Cole were still in the room I'd listened in on before.

Phaidros must've planned for this. I had to warn them. I ran through the halls as fast as I could. The palace descended into chaos. People took shelter where they could, guards trying to evacuate civilians. When they spotted me, they pivoted, trying to guide me to safety, but I shook them off.

I desperately chased the faint scent trail of Cole.

But Cole found me first.

We collided. He pushed me back just as a pillar collapsed over the spot I was about to reach.

I glanced up at him. He caged me in his arms, my back pinned against the shaking castle wall. Stark relief was splashed over his face. The childish hope that we might be okay ballooned in my chest. I wanted to believe it so, so badly.

"Cole," I gasped, barely able to speak, "I fucked up."

He teleported us away before I could explain further.

We appeared in a clearing miles away. The walls around the city were nothing more than a speck in the distance.

We escaped. But Daphne, Hecate, the citizens had remained.

"We need to go back for the others—"

My words were cut off as the ground beneath us began to shake.

I looked up at Cole in horrified confusion, but his gaze

didn't reflect the questions flashing in my mind.

"Cole, what's going on?"

There was only sorrow in his eyes when he said, "A soul for a soul."

"What does that mean?" I demanded. "So I killed Maddox. So what? I've killed before."

Cole shook his head, black hair falling in front of his eyes, obscuring those amber orbs I clung to for comfort.

"When you returned to the realm of the living, you took a life. But you're dead, Avery. There are consequences to setting the universe off balance."

Consequences. He'd told me even then, but it had been so easy to dismiss. I thought he'd meant consequences for stealing from him. Anger, yes, but not divine retribution.

The shaking beneath us grew stronger. It was hard to stay balanced.

"A soul must be taken in return." His voice was somehow soft over the roar.

"That can't be." Maddox had tried to kill me. Had tortured Daphne. And ending that life of cruelty was called *unbalanced*?

I didn't even realize I was clutching onto him in desperation until the ground behind us opened up and Cole pulled me tighter into his embrace and jumped away. It made no difference. Now that the surface had been breached, the hole chased us easily. It advanced slowly, but the void that opened beneath the ground was relentless.

"I'm going in that?" To leave behind Daphne, Hecate, the city... to leave behind Cole when I'd only found him, the other half of my soul.

But Cole shook his head.

"No."

Hope surged and died when I saw the certainty in his eyes.

"I am."

"No. You can't!" My fingers sharpened to claws, pulling his chest towards me. I cut his shirt, scratching the flesh underneath, but he didn't flinch. "We can run. You can portal us somewhere... or we can go to another realm." Surely Cole could find another Libra demon. We could escape this if we just tried.

He only shook his head. "It will never stop. Hecate was able to hide you with her magic, but it was nothing more than borrowed time."

Borrowed time. Every moment flashed before my eyes, the weeks of uncertainty with Cole, of hiding from my feelings. A waste. I'd had him for only a day when a century wouldn't be enough. Time spent training with Hecate, but what was it for if I couldn't stop this?

"It demands its due." He said the words almost tenderly. Like he knew what he was doing.

Like he knew he was breaking my heart.

"I won't let you."

I tried to call on the magic to fight the quaking ground, but my powers were dormant.

The look he gave me was something I'd never seen on Cole's face.

Pity.

My throat felt like it was shut.

"We can't fight this, little Alpha." Even now, he'd slowed his jumps, the chasm only a hundred feet away. I twisted to see it, but he pulled me back so the only thing I could see was his face.

"I need you to know, Avery... it was worth it. You own my soul. You're etched on every part of me. And if I only had you for a moment, then it was the only moment worth having in my entire lonely existence."

It was now that his mask cracked. His amber eyes were pained as the heartbreak flooded his face.

"It should be me, Cole," I pleaded.

He didn't reply, just pulled me in for one final kiss. It was searing. It was sorrowful.

I tried to summon my magic, to push him away so I could throw myself in. If ever there was a time I needed to overpower the stubborn male, it was now. Green sparks flickered on my fingers. I raised my hands as if to pull him in when I needed to push him away to distract him.

But Cole knew me as well as I knew myself.

He broke the kiss and looked down at me with infinite

tenderness. It was an expression I couldn't help but memo-
rize, a face I could never forget in thousands of years, across a
hundred lives.

"Forgive me for leaving you alone."

A whirl of dark magic that tasted like smoke and darkness teleported me away. It wasn't far, only a hundred feet. I
pushed myself up from where I'd fallen and surged forward. I
could get there. I could. I *had* to. There was no other choice.

I called on every ounce of my shifter speed, the speed I'd
never had as the weak pack Omega but that I had found in
death. The speed that should let me do this. I'd been horrified
when I thought I had to die, but if that was the price for Cole
to live, there was no contest.

Ninety feet away.

Eighty.

Seventy.

Sixty.

But I didn't even make it halfway before Cole turned and
gave me one final look. Even at the distance, I read the apology
on his face. Apology, but no regret. He wasn't sorry at all
that he was doing this. He was only sorry he was leaving me
behind.

And then he turned into the massive canyon that had
opened between us and fell in.

I'd thought his expression was what I'd remember, but it
was Cole, powerful, unstoppable Cole, falling helplessly into

the abyss that was seared in my memory.

I sprinted faster, trying to get to the part he'd fallen into. The ground repaired itself beneath my feet. New dirt and grass surged up, sealing the chasm until the clearing looked utterly undisturbed.

I fell to my knees.

An unholy wail was wrenched from my throat. I barely recognized the sound. It was pure pain.

I had died, and it had been less painful than this.

I fell against the ground, desperately clawing at the dirt. I pulled handful after handful, not caring as my nails were ruined, as one was wrenched off when I hit a rock. Blood mixed with the dirt, turning the same shade as the red sky above.

Water fell into the pit as I clawed and clawed at the ground. Tears. They barely registered.

But no matter how I pulled, how I pleaded with the ground, the sky, the Moon Goddess herself, nothing changed.

He was gone.

He was gone.

I collapsed against the ground, defeat and death strangling me in equal measures.

And I sobbed.

EPILOGUE

W HEN PEOPLE THOUGHT OF Hell, *this* was what they pictured.

The fire that burned with tireless heat, the brimstone that was suffocating in its rotten stench. But the mortal mind was not meant to comprehend the utter brutality that was existence in Tartarus.

There was nothing to do in the pits but *exist*. Exist and wish it were not so.

The fires burned and burned, lava-hot. His skin was melted and flayed and reforged against the metal shackles. His arms were pulled wide, wrenched back so his shoulders were dislodged. His legs spread below him, feet speared into opposite stones at the base of the pyre, straight through the bone. His immortal blood tried to heal him, even here, and it was a worse agony than simply letting the limb succumb to gangrene. He could not turn his head to inspect them. Sometimes, the pain was acute, vicious. Sometimes, it turned into a mind-blurring drug, and he was left unsure if his limbs were even attached. The pain wasn't gone, exactly, but rather too overwhelming for even his immortal mind to process.

Agony.

Unending agony.

But even if he could have killed himself, he would not have ended his misery.

Not when it meant she was safe.

The thought of her was the one slight balm against every cruelty Tartarus bestowed upon him.

He could barely recall her name anymore. He tried countless times each day to recall the way it rolled off his tongue, but no sound left after the first few moments. Time was different. Nothing marked the passage of it, if it even did pass. That was a kind of torture too. One second, one billion years—they felt the same.

Unending.

His own name had disappeared. He would not let himself believe he forgot her name, yet he could not utter it. He could not recall her laugh. Her smile. Only the barest hint of her essence was seared on his soul to break through the fog of torture. The exact shade of her hair. Constantly, tirelessly, he searched the flames that burned him for that exact shade.

And the flames were boundless. They covered his flesh. They stretched miles, as far as he could see, at least in the moments his eyes were able to pierce the burning smoke that came from his flesh.

How long had it been?

Did it matter?

It would never end.

Never, never, never.

Sometimes, he thought he heard the barest whisper of her voice. A cruel trick of his mind, or some proof their connection could withstand the separation?

It hadn't before.

In brief fits of sense that flashed through the growing madness, he dismissed it as a delusion brought on by raw desperation. After all, he had searched for his wife in a thousand unending nights and never glimpsed her own torture.

Maybe this was his punishment. For failing to protect her in her first life.

Better delusion than reality. He would never want her to see him like this.

He should hope she forgot him. Forget she ever met him, met him in two lives. Go on, find another love, a full life. But his selfish soul would not let him wish that kindness.

She was gentle-hearted. She was life itself.

She deserved to live.

And she didn't deserve to see how he'd failed them. How he'd failed his kingdom. How he'd failed her. Again, and again, and again.

He had gone into the abyss knowing what he would find. And knowing it meant she would not go. But the rest was left to hope—a fleeting butterfly, a worse torment than any other.

Hope that this meant she would be safe and escape the wrath of the bitch goddess.

If it was an eternity in Tartarus to guarantee her that life, so be it. He would choose to bear that abuse a thousand times over.

With her, there was never a choice.

And he had never wanted one.

Thank you for reading Forgotten Queen! If you sign up for my newsletter here, you can read about the first time Cole and Avery *really* met...
And if you're dying from that cliffhanger, be sure to read the conclusion of the Shifted Fates trilogy, *Fatal Goddess*!

ACKNOWLEDGMENTS

Forgotten Queen was a very different book for me. I've never actually written a sequel, before now let alone a full trilogy, so I'm discovering every part of Avery's story along with you. This is both an exhilarating and terrifying process. Sometimes the ending feels very clear, like in this book, but everything along the way is as much of a mystery to me as it was for you. Sometimes, I'll admit, I was scared this book wouldn't even happen. But it did. And I have a lot of people to thank for that.

Thank you to the BookTok community for embracing this book and making this publication even possible.

Thank you to Magan (Court of Spice Editing Services) and PollyAné (Proofs by Polly) for editing my messy manuscript. This book would have been impossible without you both.

Thank you to Christian (Covers by Christian) for designing a cover I love more than I ever could have imagined.

Thank you to Z for creating my first ever fantasy map.

Thank you to my friends and family for supporting me in this process, and to the writing communities I've been lucky enough to find companionship and support while bringing this book to life.

And last, but certainly not least, thank you, reader, for following me on this journey. Especially when you're rewarded with cliffhangers like that...

About the Author

Vasilisa Drake is based in New England and is constantly bouncing from city to city while she tries to find her home amidst overpriced rental apartments. Forsaken Mate is Vasilisa Drake's debut, though she's written contemporary romance under another name for several years. Fantasy romance is her first love, closely followed by pet dragons and men who are obsessed with their women. She can be found staying up way too late reading, organizing her bookshelf for the millionth time, and winning the imaginary arguments in her head at least 30% of the time.

She can be contacted via email at VasilisaDrakeBooks@gmail.com or on TikTok @VasilisaDrakeBooks

Find Vasilisa

You can find Vasilisa on several platforms including:

Bookbub

Goodreads

Instagram

Romance.io

Storygraph

TikTok